( DELPHINE PUBLICATIONS PRESENTS )

Ms. NICE
*Nasty*

AUTHOR OF *A SECRET WORTH KEEPING*

# LAKISHA JOHNSON

ISBN: 9780996174220

Edited by: Tee Marshall

Layout: Write On Promotions

Cover Design: Odd Ball Designs



Printed in the United States of America

# Dedication

*This book is dedicated to all of you who continue to believe in me! Please don't stop. Your encouragement is the fuel I need to keep writing!*

# My Thanks

The room I need to write my thanks would be another novel; however, I must thank God first, for entrusting me with such an amazing gift. I am so grateful that He doesn't limit my writing to just one genre, He simply says write, so writing is what I shall do.

To my husband, Willie, who never complains when I shut him out while I'm writing, yet, he is one of my biggest cheerleaders; thank you. To my entire family: I won't name every name, because it will take up the entire page, but please know that I love each of you for supporting me. Though, I must say thank you to my twin sister Laquisha, my cousin Nicole and my best friend Aisha, my aunt Cora and my sister Shondra who read for me and don't mind me bothering them with "how does this sound, does this flow right," type questions. I love you chicks!

To each of you who support Lakisha, the author; THANK YOU!!! I cannot believe this is my second series. How awesome is that? I would not be the author I am without readers like you who purchase my books, download my books, recommend my books and review my books. Please, don't stop believing in me!

A special heartfelt thank you to the North Memphis Library Men's Renaissance and Women's Book Club (Memphis, TN) who has supported me from the very beginning! Nothing like hometown love!

THANK YOU! THANK YOU!

# Ms. Nice Nasty

# Chapter 1

What's up y'all, it's your girl Cam! Let me stop and catch y'all up on what has been happening with me. For those of you who don't know me, my government name is Camille Holden Shannon. I am 37 years old, an attorney and married to Thomas, who is also an attorney. I'm a mother to Courtney, who is 16 and Thomas Jr., who is 15. I am a brown skin, curvy chick who loves sex. I am not shy about it and my husband knows it.

A few years ago, I secretly got involved sexually with Lyn, one of my best friends and it almost ruined my life. I got so wrapped up in the relationship that I lost myself and I almost lost my life. You have to understand; I was living carelessly during this time, partying with the girls, enjoying life and before I knew it, I was spiraling out of control.

One night, after being rejected by Lyn, I go to this motel room. I was drinking and crying, heading down a path I'd never been down. There was a young lady outside the room, who I asked to go to the liquor store for me, but instead she offered me "something" she said would make me feel better. Long story short, a week later I wake up in the hospital to find out the something she gave me was cocaine and I had almost overdosed.

Whew Lord! It was one of the worst periods of my life. One I try to forget. I overcame this troubling time with my marriage and even my friendships, including the one with Lyn, yet Chloe decides to bring it up on the last day of our vacation in Mexico last month for the holidays. She was upset, because I had offended Thomas by coming in late the night before. She's been married all of a year and now she's become the "know it all" of marriage. Yeah right! She can kiss my ass. When she's put in a few more years, then she can talk to me. Thomas has been whining and complaining a lot lately, and I am about tired of his ass too.

Anyway, enough about all that. I overcame that part of my life and I won't apologize for who I am. Like I've said before, I love sex and I don't hurt anybody to get what I want. I am not looking for another husband, a baby daddy, a girlfriend or a sugar daddy; I simply get my fix and I am out! Yeah, you can think about me what you want, call me what you please, but when you do, just call me Ms. Nice Nasty!

# Chapter 2

"Well, Cam how was the vacation with your family and friends?" Dr. Nelson asked.

"It was great, fantastic, everything that I needed."

"Can you remove your sunglasses and answer that question again with the truth this time?"

"It was good, Dr. Nelson."

"But? What aren't you telling me?

"Did Thomas call you?" I ask, removing my shades.

I knew I had my answer when he didn't say anything right away. "That motherfu..."

"He is only concerned about you, Camille."

"Oh, it's Camille now. I can't do this shit right now," I say, grabbing my purse to leave.

"Wait, hold on; stop running away every time the fire gets too hot for you to handle. You choose the situations you've been in so deal with it." He says, as someone knocks on the door. "Hold on, there's someone I want you to meet."

What the hell is going on? I think, looking at his shady ass.

"Camille Shannon, this is Dr. Melody Scott."

"And?"

"And she is going to take over your therapy sessions from now on."

"Say what now? Dude, you've got to be joking. I don't have time for all this."

"Please wait. Dr. Nelson only asked me to come so that I can help you," she says. "Why don't you give it a chance?'

"Why does everyone feel I need help? I am sick of everyone telling me what I should and shouldn't be doing. Hell, no one had an issue with my life a year ago but now everyone is concerned."

"That's only because they love you. Will you please just stay and if you don't like it, you don't have to come back."

"That's right. Please give it a try. Dr. Scott is one of my associates that I've asked to take over your sessions, because I feel that we've gotten too comfortable with each other and it's no longer helping you." Dr. Nelson says.

"Is that so?" I ask, looking at him. "Define what you mean as in too comfortable, because I never needed your help mentally, but physically, you've been a great help the last few months. Why the sudden change now?" I smile.

"Because I've been wrong Camille; I've been hurting you more than helping you and I see that now. I just hope you will let Dr. Scott help you."

"Oh, let me guess; your wife found out. No, you grew a conscience? Or did you tell one of your colleagues and they threatened to turn you in unless you turn me over to another doctor?"

"It doesn't matter Camille, the point is—"

"That's it." I laugh. "It's cool. I'll play along. You can run along Dr. Nelson, your secret is safe with me."

He leaves with his tail tucked between his legs as I sit back on the couch, looking at Dr. Scott.

"As Dr. Nelson said, my name is Dr. Melody Scott and I am a sex therapist who—"

"Get the fuck out of here!" I laugh. "Are you serious? A sex therapist."

"Yes, but hear me out. I was only asked to come because Dr. Nelson felt I could help you."

"Help me? Help me with what exactly?"

"That is what we need to find out."

"Obviously you know more about me than I know, so why don't you tell me." I say with an attitude.

"First off, lose the attitude. You ran Dr. Nelson's sessions, but I won't tolerate you running anything in here, but your mouth. You're here because deep down inside you know you need help, so cut the bullshit."

"Okay, so now that you've raised your voice, what is it that you're supposed to do for me? I only came to these little meetings to pacify my whining ass husband and to keep my job because I am great with whom I am and I don't have a problem with looking at myself in the mirror."

"I can understand you coming to keep your job but if you don't have a problem, then why are you coming to pacify your husband, because it would seem to me that you wouldn't give a damn about how he felt?"

"I value my marriage and I have an image to maintain."

"Really?" she says, laughing. "If you valued your marriage, you wouldn't be using sex as an outlet."

"I never said I did."

"You don't have to. I can look at you and tell that you're a slut. You chew men up and spit them out for fun on a good day. You use your sexuality as a weapon of mass destruction and you don't care who you leave wounded in the process. You don't care how your actions affect your marriage, because you have your husband wrapped around your finger. You're sexy and you know it and you flaunt it at every opportunity. You may not think you have a problem with the face looking back at you in the mirror, but you do, and the sooner you admit that, the better."

I start clapping. "Well bravo to you for thinking you have me all figured out, but let me tell you something Dr. Scott, I don't give a damn what you think of me. I've never asked my husband to stay where he doesn't want to be, he stays because he chooses to. Furthermore, I don't chew men up, because I don't bite nor do I use my sexuality as a weapon, because there is nothing a man can offer me that I can't get for myself. I love dick and pussy occasionally and I won't be ashamed to admit that. My husband knew what he was getting from the first day we met, shit; I slept with him on the first date, so the hell with all that. I am who I am and I won't bite my tongue in saying it. You say slut, I say Cam."

"How many men have you slept with on your job?"

"None, because I don't sleep."

"How many men have you had sex with that you work with?"

"Two."

"And you don't have a problem with that?"

"No, should I? It doesn't cause a problem with our working relationship. It's just sex. I go home to my husband and they go home to their wives."

"Yes, you should. How do you look your husband in the face after coming home from cheating? Do you feel bad at all?"

"I look at him the same way I do when I leave the house in the morning. And no, I don't feel bad, because it isn't affecting our household."

"But it is which is why you're here; you're just too selfish to recognize it."

"Yeah, whatever. Isn't our time up?"

"It is; but Camille, I hope you'll come back next Tuesday, because I am only here to help you. And Camille, I would rather help you now than later, before you've wrecked every relationship it's taken you years to build."

"Yeah, okay; I'll think about it." I say, walking towards the door. "One more thing doctor, the name is Cam."

# Chapter 3

Music playing
"Oh, come on and rock me, ooh, girl
Oh, come on and rock me, ooh, girl
Hey, girl, long time no see
Do you have a little time to spend with me?
I wanna know what's been going on
In your life, huh, talk to me, baby"

"Terrance," I call out when I don't see him in the living room.

"Hey, I didn't hear you come in."

"I know because you got your Freddie Jackson bumping. What do you know about that?"

"I know enough," He says, singing in my ear, "Ooh, girl, I'm gonna love you real good. Come on let me do it now, you know I could. I really miss the way you squeeze and moan and call out my name, woo, you can call me, baby."

"Is that so? Why don't you show me then," I say, pushing him away as I pull my shirt over my head, throwing it on the floor. He continues to sing down the hall to the bedroom and I follow as if I am headed towards the adventure of my life. I unfasten my bra and throw it on the floor as I watch him watching me. I step out of my heels as I slowly unbutton my jeans, working them off along with my panties.

"Damn, you are so sexy."

"Am I?"

"You know you are. Now come here and let me taste you. You know I've been missing your sweetness."

"Since you ask so nicely," I answer, slowly walking over to the bed. He pulls me into him and kisses me so hard I can hardly catch my breath. "Damn boy!"

He didn't say anything as he pushes me down on the bed. "Close your eyes and don't say one word."

"Now—" I start to say before he grabs my mouth.

"Not one word, Camille!" He barks.

Okay, I like this!

I feel him tie something around my wrist and then my ankle. I want to open my eyes so bad, but the suspense of what he is doing is turning me on big time! He walks around the bed and does the same thing to my other wrist and ankle, all without saying anything. Did he leave?

"Oooh," I moan as I feel something cold on my candy lady.

"Don't you dare open your eyes," he says, when he sees me raise my head.

"Shit!" I scream when he blows on my clit. He sends my mind racing before burying his head into my candy land. I go to grab his head, forgetting my hands are tied to the bed and he smiles. I am at his mercy and I love every second of it. "I'm cummmin..." I sing out as the orgasm rocks my core. I open my eyes to see who in the hell this man is because it couldn't possibly be the Terrance I knew. He has never given me an orgasm like this before.

"Untie me," I say, needing to return the favor. "Terrance, untie me."

"You're in my house, my rules!" he says as he eases his way up my body, reaching to get a condom from the nightstand.

"Baby, please! I need my hands on you."

"What did I say?" he asks as he inserts two fingers into me, quickly finding the spot to shut me up. "I can't hear you," he says, going deeper, causing me to squirt all over his hand as I scream out in ecstasy.

My wrists were tied with enough slack for him to pull me closer as he sits up on his knees to put the condom on. With my knees bent, he pushes my legs further down as he admires the work of art I possess.

"Do you even know how good this pussy is?" He asks, rubbing her slowly as he inserts and removes his finger, before placing it in his mouth. I was so hot that I needed to feel him on the inside of me and he knew it. I was squirming for his touch as he continues to play with the sweet juices seeping from her.

He grabs his rock hard cock and rubs it up against me as I was grinding into him, silently begging him to let me feel it.

"Is this what you want?" He teases, placing the head at the entrance of her lips. Slowly rising up, he pushes a little of himself in as I fight to get my arms loose. "Stop fighting." He laughs as he pushes in a little more.

"Mmm," I moan.

"You want more?" He asks, while placing his hands on the bed on each side of my head, before pushing every inch into me. I close my eyes as I moan my appreciation. "Open your eyes Camille," he demands, as he strokes life into the inside of me.

"Oh," was the only sound I can make as my girl tightens around him. He grabs the sheet on the bed as he pounds into me, hitting the spot that any man rarely reaches. His pace increases as I feel another orgasm at its peak.

"Don't stop, oh God, Terrance; don't stop!" I scream as he sits up, placing his thumb over my clit. "Shit ... shit!"

When he finally releases, he collapses on top of me.

"Damn, I should stay away from you more often." I laugh.

"What?" he asks as he unties me.

"You know what. Either you've taken some classes or you've been holding back on me."

"I can't show you everything every time. I got to keep you coming back," he says, pulling me close to him.

\*\*\*

I blink a couple of times to make out the clock on the side of the bed. 3:30 a.m. "Shit!" I say, jumping out of Terrance's bed trying to find my clothes. How in the hell did I fall asleep. I never fall sleep in another man's bed.

I didn't even say goodbye to Terrance as I quickly get dressed and ran to my car. The last thing I need is to hear Thomas' mouth.

# Chapter 4

"Another late night?"

"Thomas, please don't start."

"Don't start? My wife comes in at all times of night, or should I say morning, and you tell me not to start. I don't even know who you are anymore. Hell, our children barely see you and all you have to say is don't start."

"Yeah, don't start. I get sick of hearing you nag. Hell, that's why I don't want to come home, it's four in the morning and you want to argue."

"Shouldn't I argue with my wife when she comes in at four in the morning?"

"What do you want from me, Thomas?"

"I want you to be the wife and mother you're supposed to be. You walk around like you're single, living like nothing else matters but you. You don't give a damn about no one else feelings but Cam's."

"That's not true and you know it. I work hard to provide a comfortable lifestyle for us and I never say one word to you when you come and go as you please but as soon as I leave this house, I have to fight with you when I come back. I am tired of fighting with you and with the girls. I am tired, Thomas. Why do you think I hate coming home?"

"That's a cop out. Don't blame me for you not wanting to be at home, because I am not the problem, you are and you know it. This home hasn't changed; you have and if you would stop for a minute to look around, you'd see that. You are thirty-seven years old, a partner in your law firm, with two teenage children, friends and family who love you, yet you are pushing everybody away."

"How am I pushing everybody away?"

"You know how?"

"No, tell me. Since you seem to know everything, tell me how."

"By not caring."

"I do care. How can you honestly look me in my face and tell me I don't care about my family and friends. I'll do anything for y'all."

"Except get the help you need."

"What is that supposed to mean? I am still going to therapy, because you think that's what I need. Isn't that getting the help you think I need? Dr. Nelson told me you called."

"I did call him, because face it, Cam, you have some demons that you need to deal with and if you don't, you will wake up one day with nothing and nobody. You are going to therapy, but you don't seem to be getting anything out of it."

"And what exactly is it that you think I need Thomas?"

"You need to start valuing me as your husband."

"Okay, so when are you starting therapy?"

"For what?"

"To start valuing me as your wife?"

"I do value you. Why do you think I am fighting so hard for you to get better?"

"Got damn it!" I yell. "What do I need to get better from? I am not dying. I am sick of everybody having an opinion about Cam, when none of you have ever walked in my shoes. Yes, I make it look easy, but none of you know. You want to act like I've completely changed, when I've always been this way. You knew who you were getting when you married me."

"Stop acting like you're a victim. You act like you're the only one providing the means for our family to eat and you're not. You act like you had a rough childhood, when you didn't. Yes, I knew who I was marrying, yet she isn't the same woman I see standing before me. The woman I married would never carry on like you are. You do need to get better, because you can't even see that the shit you're doing is affecting our home."

"Carrying on like what, Thomas? What am I doing that is affecting our home, sir? The last time I checked, nothing has changed in this house. All of the bills are being paid. Your clothes are being washed. Your dick is being sucked. You are eating. So what's lacking? I am sick of all you motherfuckers. You keep saying that I may wake up without anybody, when you need to understand that you might be the one waking up without me. I'm going to take a shower and then I'm going to bed."

"Run like you always do, but remember this, one of these days we might not be here when you decide to return."

"And you might find that I don't care."

15

# Chapter 5

"Hey Stephanie," I say the next morning, walking into work.

"Hey boss lady, welcome back. How was your vacation?"

"It was great. How was everything around here? You know it's been forever since I've taken an entire month off."

"I know, but everything here was good. You didn't miss a thing. I've already loaded your schedule to your iPad and I started the coffee in your office."

"Great, thank you."

It felt weird being back in the office after a long vacation, but here no one judges me, because Camille the attorney is fierce. Hell, I've always known I would be an attorney after watching my mom and dad in courtrooms all of my life.

"Mrs. Shannon," Stephanie said, drawing me out of my thoughts. "Do you want me to fix you a cup of coffee?"

"No, I can get it."

"Okay. And Mr. Townsend called and wants to see you in his office at ten AM."

"Did he say the reason?"

"No ma'am."

"Okay. Thanks Stephanie. Can you close the door on your way out?"

I pulled out my iPad to look over my schedule for today. There was a new client coming in at 12 to discuss a merger she is looking to close, but other than that, it seems to be an easy day. I turn on my laptop and rearrange my desk as I prepare to meet with the head of our firm, Mr. Milton Townsend.

I quickly go over some emails and I see one from Lyn from two weeks ago. That's weird. We were all together on vacation. I click on it and its pictures of me while on vacation. One is of me standing by the pool. I hadn't even realized she took it. I look damn good in my bikini, but it's still kind of weird. Another one is of me and her, a selfie we took at a restaurant. Okay, this is creepy. I didn't look at any of the other pictures, because I had to go to my meeting.

"Mr. Townsend, you want to scc me?" I say, pushing his door open to see Judge Alton sitting in his office.

"Yes, Mrs. Shannon, come in. You know Judge Charles Alton, don't you?"

"Yes, I've had the privilege of having her. In my courtroom, I mean." Charles says, smiling.

"It's good to see you again, Judge," I say, giving him a sly look. "What can I do for you gentlemen this morning?"

"Have a seat. Do you want anything to drink?"

"No, I'm fine."

"Mrs. Shannon, while you were on vacation, Judge Sumner became ill and has decided to step down from the bench."

17

"Ill? Is she okay?" I ask.

"No, she has terminal cancer and she won't be able to handle the term she was just voted into, so she decided to vacate the seat."

"I am so sorry to hear that. What does that have to do with me?"

"You've been nominated to fill her seat." Mr. Thompson says.

"Wait, what?"

"Camille, you are a great attorney as it is evident in your work and we both know that you would make a damn good judge." Judge Alton adds.

"Uh," I say, sitting back in my chair, "wow, this is a great opportunity but I was thinking I had another few years to prepare for this. How did this happen?"

"Your work spoke for you."

"Look Camille, if we didn't think you could handle it, we wouldn't be having this conversation. Your name has already been given to the Tennessee Judicial Nominating Committee as a candidate for the position. All you have to do is fill this questionnaire out." Mr. Townsend says.

"And what now?"

"Once you fill out the questionnaire, the Judicial Committee will select three names from the pool of candidates and submit their selection to the governor. Afterwards, he will make his pick. He has sixty days to decide."

"That's it?" I ask.

"That's it."

"Wow. Thank you!"

"You don't have to thank us Camille. We believe you would be the best woman for the job. It's in your district and you are more than qualified for it. Yes, it came a few years before you thought it would, but it's here now; don't pass on the chance. "

"Wow!" I say, getting up from my chair. "This is an amazing opportunity and it would be crazy for me to pass on it, but I do have sixty days before a decision is made, right?"

"A decision can be made at any time and once the decision is made, you can decide then if you want the position. If you do, you will be sworn in to take over the remaining of the term left by Judge Sumner until election time."

"So, for the next eight years?"

"Yes."

"And you both recommended me?"

"Yes. We have no doubt that you can do this." Judge Alton said.

"Well thank you gentlemen for having such great confidence in me. You don't know how much this means to me."

"Just make us proud."

# Chapter 6

When I got back to my office, I was still in shock over what just happened. I pick up my phone to call Thomas, when there was a knock on my door.

"Come in."

"Hey," Charles says, coming in and closing the door behind him.

"I thought you were still with Mr. Townsend."

"No, I have an appointment to get to, but I wanted to stop by here first."

"What made you all think of me for filling Judge Sumner's seat?"

"You're the best person for the job."

"I'm still in shock though. This is huge, Charles."

"It is, but you can handle it."

"I know I can, but it's still a shock no less, a huge shock!"

"Listen, I have a meeting that I have to get to. Why don't you meet me for dinner tonight and we can discuss it more," he says, walking around my desk.

"I can't tonight, but how about Sunday? Um, you smell so good."

"And so do you and this skirt?"

"I thought you had a meeting to get to."

"I do and this is the only reason I don't have you over your desk right now," he says, kissing me on my neck and putting his hand under my skirt.

I unbuckle his belt and pants releasing him. "Don't you have a meeting?"

"It can wait."

Sucking his tongue into my mouth, I push his pants down as he works to remove my thongs.

I push him down in the chair, raising my skirt as I prepare to sit for a minute. I turn my back to him as I rub my lady to make sure she is ready. It's been over a month since I've seen Charles, so I knew this wouldn't last long, I had a meeting at twelve. I bend and grab his hard cock as I slide down. "Hmm."

"Mmm," he moans.

I put my hands on the desk and my feet flat on the floor as I ride him forming circles with my pelvis, making sure he feels all of me.

He grabs my waist and I cover his hands as he releases inside of me. I lean back into him.

"I've missed you," he says.

Laughing, I say, "I bet you did." I get up as we both go into my office bathroom.

"Dinner on Sunday," he says before kissing me goodbye.

When he leaves, I sit back down to call Thomas, but decide to call my dad instead. It had been over a month since I've talked to him. We used to be so close, but with them living in Miami and me in Memphis, the distance makes it hard.

"Judge Holden's office, how may I help you?"

"Judge Holden, please."

"May I ask your name?"

"Camille Shannon."

"One moment please."

"Camille, is this really you?"

"Yes, Daddy; how are you?"

"I am great now that I'm hearing your voice. I thought you disappeared into thin air. Where have you been?"

"Just working, you know how it is. How is Mom?"

"She is your mom, do you even have to ask. Is everything okay with you?"

"Yes, I just wanted to hear your voice and I want to talk to you about something."

"Okay, what is it?"

"I've been nominated to fill the seat of a judge, who had to step down in my district."

"Wow baby, that's great, but why don't you sound excited about it?"

"I just don't know Daddy. I know how it was when you were elected. People dig into every aspect of your life and right now, that is the last thing Thomas and I need."

"What do you mean? Has something happened that I need to know about?"

"No Daddy, it's just the usual drama that happens in any marriage."

"Are you sure? Don't make me come up there, because you know I will."

I start laughing, "No macho man, calm down. I am excited about, it's just shocking."

"Well, if there is anybody that I know can handle it, you can."

"Thanks Dad. Listen, I have a meeting, but I do want to talk to you about this some more tonight, okay? Tell Mom I said hi and I will call you later."

"I look forward to it. I love you."

"I love you too Daddy."

As soon as I hung up, Stephanie was buzzing to let me know my new client was here.

"Send her in, please." I say, while pulling up her case file on my iPad.

"Mrs. Shannon," she says, walking in.

"Yes, and you are Mrs. Walker, right?"

"Yes. Thank you for taking my case on such short notice."

"No problem." I say, looking her over. She was gorgeous. "I've read over the paperwork that was sent, but why don't you tell me why you're here."

"Well, I've recently taken over my father's company, Donnington & Associates, and I'm looking for a new firm to represent us. In the midst of this, there is a merger that I couldn't put off until a new firm was in place, so I am hoping you can assist us with all of the legal issues that comes with taking over another company."

"I see. So your company buys smaller companies or companies that are in jeopardy of closing, in order to save them from going under."

"Yes, and with my father's sudden death, there are a lot of things he had in the works that I am now trying to finish."

"I am sorry to hear about your father. Is this merger new and what happened to your previous firm?"

"No, this merger is almost complete, but the old firm and I can't seem to see eye to eye on the final details, so I thought it would be best to get my own, new representation."

"You sound like a very smart business woman."

"I wish everyone would think like that. All they see is a sexy woman in five-inch heels and a skirt and they instantly think I don't know anything."

"That's because they expect us to use what's under our skirts and not our brains."

"Yes, I am realizing that now since all of this has been dropped in my lap. Anyway, I brought you the contract and all of the information I have on this company, in order for you to know more before you decide to take it. I am actually flying down to Miami to meet with the board next Wednesday, if you would like to join me."

"Let me meet with the other partners to go over the case and I will call you later today and let you know."

"Great. It was nice meeting you and I look forward to working with you."

"Likewise," I say, as I watch her walk out. Damn!

# Chapter 7

I spent the next few hours working on the contract that Mrs. Walker left. Some things weren't adding up, so I asked the firm's investigator to look into them, before I planned to meet with the other partners tomorrow morning. I was getting ready to pack up when my cell phone vibrated on the desk. I put it on speaker.

"Hey, Ray."

"Don't hey me. Why haven't I heard from your raggedy ass? I haven't heard or seen you since we got back from vacation. What did you guys do for the New Year?"

"I did someone's son. What did you do?"

"I should have known. I partied with Anthony and the kids of course, but how are you? What are you up to?"

"I'm good girl, about to leave the office. How are you?"

"I can't complain. I'm headed over to Shelby's house to hang out with the girls."

"No!"

"I haven't even asked you anything yet," she says, laughing.

"I already know what you're going to ask and I don't feel like being judged by them tonight. I have enough of that at home."

"Cam, come on now. You know how those hoes are. Stop wearing your feelings on your sleeve. We've said worse things to each other."

"I know Ray, but I just don't feel like it tonight. I have a lot on my mind, so I'm just going to call it a night."

"What?" she asks, sounding like she was choking. "You are calling it a night and going home as in your house?"

"Shut up wench! Don't act like this is something new."

"Is everything okay? And don't lie either, because I will be at your house before you get there."

"Yes honey, I am fine. There is something I need to talk to Thomas about first and then I will tell you, okay?"

"Something bad?"

"No, actually, it's great, but I want to tell him and the kids first, because he is always whining that I tell you everything first."

"You are supposed to, but okay, let's meet for breakfast Saturday. How about nine-ish at the Waffle House we normally go to."

"That would be great."

"Do you want me to mention it to the others?"

"Yeah, that'll be cool."

"Okay, I'll see you then."

"Thanks Ray."

***

"Hey Mom!" Courtney says when I finally make it in the house.

"Hey baby. What are you up to?"

"Trying to find something to eat."

26

"Where are your brother and dad?"

"They are watching a game in the den."

"Okay, well let's order some take out."

"Chinese or pizza?"

"It doesn't matter to me. You know what I like. Go and ask the guys while I change clothes."

"Hey, I didn't know you were home."

"Hey," I say to Thomas as I stand in the closet, changing into some sweat pants and shirt.

"Is everything okay?"

"Yeah, why do you ask?"

"Because you're home for dinner."

"Thomas, can I ever do anything right? If I am not home, you have a problem and even when I am, you still have one."

"I'm sorry. I don't want to argue with you. Please accept my apology, because I came in wrong. Are you okay?" he asked, walking over to give me a hug.

"I'm just tired Thomas. Tired of fighting in our home. I fight in courtrooms every day and I don't want to do it when I get home. I know I've made some mistakes, but can you please give me some slack?"

"I get it and I'm sorry. Can we just have a nice dinner tonight?"

"Yes, please! I'll be down in a minute."

"Hey Mom," TJ says, running to give me a hug.

"Hey, how was your day today?"

"It was good."

27

"The food is here," Courtney yells from the kitchen.

"Courtney you did a good job on ordering the food, because I am starving. I didn't get a chance to eat lunch today."

"Me neither," Thomas says, stuffing his mouth with food. "I have a new client that kept me tied up for four hours."

"Really, I didn't think you were taking any new clients."

"I wasn't, but this client was referred to me by the mayor, so I couldn't turn it down."

"Um, okay. Since we are all here, there are two things I want to talk to you all about. First, I have a new client who needs me at a meeting in Miami next week, so I will be gone for a few days. Since I will be down there, I thought I would visit my parents."

"Can we go? We haven't seen Granddaddy in months?" Courtney asks.

"Seeing that you all just went back to school from holiday break, I don't want you all to miss another two days from school."

"Come on Mom!"

"Let me think about it and I'll check with your teachers to see if it'll be okay for you all to miss before I agree."

"Why do you want to visit your parents all of a sudden?"

"Because I haven't seen them and since I have to go anyway, why not. What's the problem?"

"Well, I can't go. With this new client, I can't leave now, but don't let me stop you all from going."

Rolling my eyes, I say, "Anyway. The other thing is, when I got to work this morning, I had a meeting with my boss and my name has been placed in the hat to fill the seat of Judge Sumner, who had to step down due to illness."

"Really Mom! That's great." Courtney says.

"Yeah, that is great news. My mom as a judge would be so cool."

"Judge Sumner. She is the one who has cancer, right? Have you decided to do it?" Thomas asks cutting off the children's excitement.

"I haven't decided anything yet, because it's not an actual decision that I make. The governor has to choose between me and two other people."

"And if you are chosen?"

"If?"

"Dang Dad, you act like you don't want Mom to take this job? Aren't you excited for her?" Courtney asks.

"I'm just asking if you have already made your mind up, or if we have any say in it?" he asks.

"No, my mind hasn't been made up, but I would hope that a once in a lifetime opportunity like this, something that I've worked hard for, for all of my adult life; would be something my husband wouldn't need to think about me accepting."

"Yeah, okay," he says.

"Can we be excused?"

"Yes. Go ahead. Thanks for ordering dinner, it was great."

"Man, you are a piece of work," I say when the kids leave the table.

"Me?" he laughs.

"Yes. What's your problem with me taking this position?"

"I didn't say I had a problem with you taking this position, but I have a problem with you making a decision that can affect this family on your own like you always do."

"Did you not hear me just tell you about the fucking position? Did you not hear me say I found out about it this morning, when I got back to work from vacation?"

"You don't have to curse."

"Obviously I do, because you can't hear otherwise. Damn! I can't do anything right with you," I say, getting up to put my plate in the dishwasher.

# Chapter 8

I leave the house early in order to get to the office to get a jump-start on the new case I received yesterday. Having to meet with the partners and then having to travel to Miami on next week, I want to be prepared for what I was walking into. I decide to stop by this little coffee shop I liked called Republic Coffee first, to get myself together after the conversation last night with Thomas. I find a spot in the corner and place my order as I pull my iPad out.

"Cam?" I hear someone call my name.

"Lyn?"

"Hey girl, how are you?"

"I am good. How are you?" I ask, looking a little shocked to see her.

"I am better now that I've seen you. Did you ever get the email I sent you?" she asks, sitting across from me.

"Email?"

"Yeah, from our vacation."

"Oh, yeah. I haven't had a chance to look through all the pictures, but I've meaning to ask you about those. Why were you taking pictures of me anyway?"

"I was taking pictures of everybody, but you were looking fine as wine in those bikinis."

"Uh, thank you, but what brings you to this neck of the woods?" I ask.

"I was hoping to run into you."

"Run into me? So what, you sit here every morning, hoping I would stop in?"

"Something like that."

"Okay, this is weird. What the hell is going on, Lyn?" I ask.

"I've been trying to talk to you since we were in Mexico."

"Talk to me about what?"

"Us."

"Us? There is no us."

"There could be."

"Okay, I'm being setup, right? Where are the other girls?" I ask, looking around. "Who put you up to this?"

"I'm serious Cam. I miss you," she says as the waitress comes over with my coffee and cheese grits.

"I'm sorry, but can you make this to go?" I ask her as I pack up my shit.

"Cam, please don't leave."

"Yes, I am, because either you're crazy or I am if you think I'm about to entertain this foolishness. What makes you think I want a relationship with you?"

"You've had one before."

"Yeah and it almost cost me my life."

"It can be different this time."

"There is no this time, Lyn. What is wrong with you?"

"There is nothing wrong with me. Why do people keep asking me that?"

"Who else has asked you that?"

"Paul, Kelsey, Ray, Shelby and now you."

"Lyn, I am only going to say this once; there is no us and there isn't a chance that there will be. I don't know where you are getting this, but don't come at me like this again."

I grab my things, walk up to the counter, pay for my breakfast, and leave her sitting there.

I make it to the office and was getting settled when my investigator Raul comes in.

"Cam, I've checked into Monica Walker and she has checked out. Do you want me to proceed with looking into Donnington and Associates?"

"Yes. I want to know whom we are getting involved with, before I decide to take on this case. Then we need to look into the company they are trying to buy. All of their information is in the case."

"Okay. I will have some information to you this evening."

"Thanks Raul. I have a meeting this morning with the partners."

***

I was still in my office and it was almost ten pm. I had my shoes off, my feet up on the couch, and papers everywhere, but I was too tired to drive home. My mind was still playing back the shit that happened this morning with Lyn. I've been meaning to call Shelby and Ray, but I've been so busy that I haven't had the chance. With so much on my mind, I grab my phone and turn on my Bluetooth, so that I could play some music through the speakers I had set in my office. I grab my remote and turn the lights down. Damn I love this office. I hit shuffle and "Chocolate Legs" by Eric Benet start to flow.

I close my eyes, trying to think of someone to call who can sex me up, before I go home and I begin rubbing on my own chocolate legs. I rub down between them, my girl is already hot and I know she's wet, so I let my finger slide inside my panties. With my other hand, I start to play with my breast. I stop long enough to pull my skirt up and take my panties off. I place one leg on the back of the couch, and the other on the edge of the table as my fingers find the spot yearning for a touch. I put my fingers in and then bring them to my lips to taste my own sweetness. Damn girl! Placing my wet fingers back into my candy box, I feel her throbbing for a release. Taking my time, I rub her. Slowly inserting two fingers in and gyrating from the sensation it was sending through my body, I can feel my juices running onto the couch as my strokes became harder and faster. Pushing my fingers deeper, I feel my orgasm forming and I can no longer control it. As she squirts, my body shakes and I cry out, making myself smile at the reaction I can cause myself.

"Damn!"

I jump when I hear a voice. "How long have you been standing there?"

"Long enough to see that you have skills."

"Care to join me?"

"Oh no, I am strictly dickly."

"And? That's what they all say at first."

When she couldn't say anything, I lower my legs and get up to get a towel from the bathroom. "Cat got your tongue?" I ask when I walk by. I intentionally walk close enough for her to smell my aroma on my breath.

Clearing her throat, she says, "No, I'm good."

"Then what brings you to my office this time of night Mrs. Walker? I mean Monica?"

"I tried calling you, but I got the answering service. I pass this way headed home, so I decided to stop and the security guard said you were still here."

"That still doesn't answer my question."

"Well, I received some news from my private investigator about Brunson Manufacturing."

"The company you're trying to save?" I ask, while putting my panties back on and fixing my skirt.

"Yes."

"Have a seat," I tell her, pointing to the chair across from me. "Now what did he find?"

"Well for starters, this company is a front for a major drug cartel in Miami. He is trying to get a legitimate company to take it over, because the Feds are investigating him."

"Wow, okay and your old law firm couldn't find this out?"

"They knew, but they didn't care, because it was more money in their pocket. I knew I didn't like them and this further proves my point."

"So what's next?"

"For starters, the trip to Miami is canceled. Next, I would like to retain your firm as our lead legal team and then I want to have our books and everything audited."

"Are you sure? It may dig up some stuff on your dad."

"Yes, I'm sure. If there are any unethical business practices going on, I will shut the doors of Donnington and Associates. My husband and I have worked too hard to allow this to tear everything we have apart. I never wanted this damn company anyway, but Dad left it to me in his will."

"Well, we will be happy to take over your legal obligations. I have my investigator Gabe checking out your company and this company was next on the list anyway, because I wanted to know what I was walking into and I am glad to know that we were thinking alike. What do you and your husband do?"

"My husband is District Attorney Brent Walker and I am an author."

"You're an author? I never would have guessed it."

"Yes, I have a few best sellers out and a new one being released in a few weeks. I'm actually having a release party coming up next month; I'll send you the invitation."

"Great. Can I bring my girls?"

"Of course. Look, I'm not going to hold you any longer. I'm sorry about changing your plans at the last minute, but I am glad we found this out now before I signed that contract."

"It's no problem. I'm still going to Miami to visit my parents."

"Great, then it all worked out. Thank you Mrs. Shannon."

"Girl we are way past that, you can call me Cam."

"Thank you Cam and I'll be looking for you at the party."

"I will be there."

When she left, I was trying to figure out where I knew her husband from. I went online to Google his name and as soon as his picture came up, I instantly remembered him from a party the girls and I went to with Judge Alton. This should be fun. I thought, as I shut my computer down to head home.

# Chapter 9

*Breakfast with the Girls*

"Hey boo, I am so happy to see you," Ray said, giving me a hug when I finally make it to Waffle House.

"Hey," I say, sliding into the booth.

"Well dang, that's all I get?"

"I'm sorry Ray. I just have so much on my mind."

"Good morning ladies. What can I get you to drink?"

"Coffee for me, please."

"Me as well."

"I'll take coffee too," Shelby says, coming in.

"Oh my God Shelby, look at this stomach." I say getting up to hug her, since I hadn't seen her since I left Mexico.

"How are you Cam, I've missed you."

"I am good and it looks like you are too. How are you and Derrick?"

"I am. We are good. We got married two weeks ago at the justice of the peace and now we are just waiting the arrival of this little one."

"Married and you didn't tell me?"

"You wouldn't answer my calls, remember?"

"I know and I am sorry. Can you please forgive me?"

"Of course I can. Now, how have you been?"

"Uh, I've been better."

"What's wrong?"

"Thomas. Do I have to say anything more?"

"Are you ladies ready to order?" the waitress asks.

After ordering our food, we went back to our conversation.

"So what is up with Thomas?"

"I really don't know. He complains because I'm not at home, and then complains when I am."

"Have you tried talking to him?"

"Girl, between him and therapy, I am talked out. Shit! Anyway, enough about him; a few days ago at work, I got some great news. I've been selected as a candidate to fill Judge Sumner's circuit court seat in my district."

"Oh my God, Cam, that is amazing. What did you say?"

"Well, I haven't said anything yet, because I haven't officially been chosen. It's up to the governor and he has sixty days to make his choice."

"Who are you up against?" Shelby asks.

"I don't know. The names of the other nominees are not known. I didn't even know my name was in the hat, until Mr. Thompson and Charles told me."

"Charles, as in your boo Charles?" Ray asks.

"Yes."

"Well, you are one hell of an attorney and I know you will rock as a judge, so you got this."

"Girl, I just don't know if I am ready for this. You know as soon as I am selected, the media will be all up in my business, trying to find out who the hell Camille Shannon is."

"And? She ain't that bad? That Cam bitch though! They better watch out for her." Ray says, laughing.

"Ray, you are a fool!" Shelby says as she bites into the chocolate chip waffle the waitress sits on the table. "Seriously, Cam, you can't allow your fear to hold you back. You are a great attorney and obviously your boss feels the same way, or he wouldn't have put his name on the line to get you nominated."

"I hear what both of you are saying and you're right. This is so surreal though."

"Have you talked to your dad about it?" Ray asks.

"Yes and he is so excited; I'm actually taking the kids to see my parents next week, so we will talk then."

"Well if there is anybody who can get you to do what is right, it's Daddy Holden." Shelby laughs.

"I know right. I can remember the spring breaks and summers we spent down there while in college. Hell, he still scares me," Ray adds.

"You are right, which is why I have to talk to him before I make any decision."

"When are you all leaving?"

"Tuesday, after the kids get out of school."

"Is your mom excited? I know it's been a while since you've been home."

"She is very excited, but I think it has more to do with seeing the kids. Anyway, when is this little one due Shelby?"

"August twelfth; that date can't get here fast enough. Between Derrick and Brenae's terrible two's; this has felt like the longest pregnancy and I'm only four months."

"Yeah boo, you have a few more months." I laugh. "Oh, but I've got to tell you both about this weird run-in I had with Lyn."

"Lyn? Where did you see her at?"

"She was waiting for me at the coffee shop over off Walnut Grove."

"Waiting for you?"

"Yes. This heifer started talking crazy, saying stuff like she wants to be with me and misses me. At first I thought y'all had put her up to it, so I started looking around like she was messing with me, but when I realized she was serious, I told her she needed help and I got the hell away from her."

"I told you, Shelby."

"I know Ray but—" Shelby says.

"But what?" I ask. "What is going on?"

"She has been acting very strange lately and all she talks about is you."

"Me? Why? She did mention that she was tired of everybody saying she needs help."

"I don't know, but stay away from her Cam." Ray says.

"Don't worry. She even sent me some pictures that she took of me while we were on vacation. I mean, this is some weird shit y'all."

"I don't know what is going on with her, but I think I am going to reach out to Paul to see if he knows."

"Okay and please let me know. Anyway, how are the other girls? I haven't spoken to any of them since we came back from vacation."

"Kerri and Mike are expecting their second baby in July; Chloe and Todd are doing great. Todd is opening up his third restaurant tonight. You should have received an invitation to the grand opening. You are coming?" Shelby asks.

"I have so many emails, I probably overlooked it. I will call her and maybe stop through."

"That will be good, because everyone was really upset with the way things were left. You do know that we love you and we aren't judging you, right?"

"Yes, I know and I was so caught up in my feelings that I couldn't see straight and I do apologize for ignoring you." I said to Shelby. "Ray, what's up with you and Anthony?"

"Girl, fuck Anthony!"

"Well damn, that bad?"

"He just gets on my nerves. I love his bald head ass, but shit!"

"Is he still taking care of the ex-wife?"

"No, he finally cut ties with all of that once he realized I was for real about being done with him. I know he is still financing her care, which I have no problem with, but that's it."

"How is Justin?"

"His bitch ass is alright! Hell, he gets on my nerves too."

"Ray, your ass is crazy."

"I'm serious. I want to slap him and Anthony most days."

"What about you Cam? Is everything really alright with you?"

"No, but it's getting there. Oh, check this out; Dr. Nelson bought in another therapist for me to see. A sex therapist because they feel I use sex as an outlet for my issues. Can you believe that?"

When neither of them said anything, I said, "Um, hello?"

"Well, you are the freakiest person I've ever met. I wouldn't say that you use sex as an outlet, you just like sex."

"So are you saying I have a sex addiction?"

"Can you stop having sex whenever you want? Can you go weeks without it?"

"Yes and no. Weeks? Hell no, a bitch will be dried up by then."

"I'm with her, Shelby. I can't even go weeks." Ray says.

"See, I'm not the only one."

"Yeah, okay that just means both of y'all are addicted."

"Whatever." Ray said grabbing her purse. "I hate to rush, but I have to pick Rashida up from driving school."

"Thank you guys for coming. I might see you all tonight at the grand opening. If not, I will call as soon as I get back, so we can plan something."

"Sounds good to me. If we don't see you, have a safe trip."

# Chapter 10

"How was your breakfast?"

"Do you really want to know Thomas, or are you trying to see if that is where I really went?"

"I just asked you a question. I don't want to fight with you this morning."

"And I don't want to fight with you either," I said, pulling the covers off the bed to change them.

"Look Cam, I know this last year hasn't been the greatest for us, but I want things to get back on track. I love you and I only want the best for you," he said, walking up behind me and turning me around. "Do you believe me?"

"I've never doubted your love Thomas, it's just the way you treat me most times."

"Let me apologize to you right now; I make a vow to do better and I am sorry about last night. I am very proud of you and I know you will make a kick-ass judge."

"Thank you; I apologize for my actions lately and I will do better too."

"I really am sorry baby. I love you," he says, kissing me.

"Do you?" I laugh.

"Yes, very much."

"Not judging by that kiss."

"Damn! You got something better Miss Judge?"

"Yeah, let me show you," I say, kneeling in front of him and pulling his shorts down before pushing him back on the bed. I grab his growing cock in my hand as I lick the head, sucking him into my mouth. I open my mouth to allow some saliva to slide down the sides as I use my tongue to make circles around it. I push it in until it touches the back of my throat. I release him and quickly take him back in before he could even blink. I suck hard while massaging his balls.

"Damn girl, I've missed this," he says, running his hand through my hair. "Suck this d—" He starts to say, before I make him lose his thoughts. I feel him tightening up, which means he is close to his peak. I remove him from my mouth and stand up to step out of my jogging pants.

I climb on him in the sixty-nine position again, taking him into my mouth as he takes me into his. He sucks so hard on my clit that it makes me tighten my jaws around him.

I couldn't take anymore, so I climb off him and turn around to mount. Sliding down slowly, I got chills. You have to understand, Thomas and I never have a problem in bed, because he satisfies me sufficiently, but it's when we're not in bed that all hell breaks loose.

"Oooh," I moan, picking up my pace as he grabs my waist, moaning his satisfaction.

He pulls me close, kissing me while inserting his tongue into my mouth. I suck on his tongue while gyrating on his dick, which causes me to cum so hard.

"Baby, you feel so good," I moan into his mouth.

I sit up to ride him into his orgasm while he grips my waist.

"Uh," he moans, as I continue without stopping, causing him to empty inside of me.

"Damn that was good," I say, falling next to him on the bed.

"I know. I wish our entire relationship was as good as the sex we have."

"Me too but—"

"Mom, I need some money!" Courtney screams from downstairs.

"And life resumes," I say, getting up to put my pants back on. "Can we finish this conversation later?"

"Of course and I'll finish changing the sheets."

"Little girl, why are you yelling," I say, coming downstairs. "Oh, hey Kelsey; I didn't know you were here. When do you go back to school?"

"Hey Auntie. I leave on Tuesday."

"I was yelling because I need some money to go to the mall with Kelsey."

"Kelsey, how is your mom?"

"I don't know Auntie. She hasn't been acting herself lately."

"I know because I saw her the other day. Tell your dad to give me a call, and if you need anything, you call me."

"Okay."

"Money please."

"Don't rush me!" I say, pushing Courtney on the way to get my purse.

"Thank you ma'am."

"I got your ma'am. Y'all be safe and text me on your way home."

"Okay," Courtney says.

"I'm serious Courtney. Come straight home."

I went back upstairs to shower and change clothes.

"Oh, you actually changed the sheets."

"Oh shut up!" Thomas says, throwing a pillow at me. "What are your plans for today?"

"I don't have any really. Shelby said Todd's grand opening of his new restaurant is tonight. If you want to go, we can."

"That's cool."

"Okay, I'll find the invitation or call Chloe for the details. I was going to go by the mall to find something to wear and maybe some lunch. What do you have planned?"

"A date with my wife, if she'd let me."

"Wait, what?"

"Why did you say it like that? This is stuff we used to do all the time, until we let life get in the way."

"I know. I was just shocked. It's been forever since you've wanted to go shopping with me. I don't mind, trust me, I was just shocked. Let me shower and change. Where is TJ?"

"He's over Chris' house."

"Okay. Give me thirty minutes."

# Chapter 11

"I must say, I've really enjoyed hanging with you today."

"Dang, you act like you've never enjoyed it before."

"You know what I mean. It's been a while since we've done anything like this."

"I know what you mean; I was just messing with you," he says, grabbing my hand as we prepare to leave the restaurant from having lunch.

"Let me go to the bathroom first. Then we have to get home so I can find something to wear to the grand opening, since we didn't make it to the mall."

I talked to Chloe earlier and got all of the details and I was excited about seeing her and Todd tonight. I didn't tell her that I was coming for sure, because I want to surprise her. Coming out of the bathroom, I didn't see Thomas at the table, so I walk to the front, only to see him arguing with somebody I couldn't make out, outside the door. Walking out, I realize its Chelle, the chick we've had a few threesomes with. Clearing my throat, I surprise them.

"Cam, uh Cam," he says, stuttering.

"Yeah, that's my name and now that we've established that, what in the hell is going on?"

"Nothing, I ran into Chelle while I was waiting on you to come out."

"And you expect me to believe that, with you looking like you're about to choke at any second?"

"Nawl baby, I'm good. You ready to go?" he asks, trying to grab my hand.

"Hell no, I want to know what the fuck you two are arguing about. I asked you first, but since you want to act like I'm stupid, Chelle would you care to explain?"

"I'm pregnant."

"Congratulations, now what does that have to do with my husband?"

"Ask him," she says, smiling.

"Why would I need to ask him when you made the statement? Both of y'all are starting to piss me the fuck off, so I don't give a damn who answers me, but one of you motherfuckers better say something."

"Cam, it's not what you think."

"Um, I'm not thinking anything, which is the reason I asked one of you simple bastards to tell me. So Thomas, I am going to ask you one last time, what does Chelle being pregnant have to do with you?"

"Babe, please just listen. She says the baby is mine."

"How far along are you?" I ask Chelle.

"Two months."

"How could the baby be yours, when it's been six months since we've seen her?"

"Uh, see—"

"You're stuttering now? Spit it out!"

"I've been with her without you and we used protection, but I guess it broke or something, because now she's telling me this is my baby."

"And how long have you known?"

"He's known for—" Chelle started to say, until I gave her a "shut the hell up" look.

"She told me two weeks ago."

"And how long have you all been sleeping together?"

"Since the last time we were all together."

"Wow," I say, walking to the car.

"Wait, Cam, please."

"Wait?" I say laughing. "Are you fucking kidding me? You want me to stand here and talk after finding out you've got our sidepiece pregnant. Yeah, okay; wait on it. You better hope I don't run your bitch ass over."

I leave him and her standing there, because had I not, I could possibly end up in jail for triple homicide. I make it home in less than twenty minutes. I tend to drive fast when I'm mad. I was just glad the kids were not home. They both called while we were eating, asking to spend the night out. I didn't really like the fact of Courtney staying at Lyn's house, but I couldn't tell her that. I storm in the house slamming doors and shit, because I was beyond pissed.

Fifteen minutes later, I hear Thomas coming through the front door.

"Cam!" He screams. "Cam, where are you?"

He finally finds me in my closet. "Cam, will you please just listen to me?"

"Listen to you?" I say, taking a sip of the drink I fixed as I throw clothes around.

51

"You've been treating me like shit lately and this entire time you've been sleeping with Chelle. This whole fucking time!"

"What do you want me to say?"

"Really? You're asking me? You should know what to say. Find the balls you used to get her pregnant and use them now, because you need to say something."

"I never meant for this to happen. Hell, I never meant for this to even go this far. I saw her one night I was out and it was around the time you weren't coming home and—"

"Oh, so let me get this straight. I'm the reason you went out, slept with someone else without a condom, and produced a child? Very original, Thomas."

"That's not what I meant. I made a mistake Chelle, I mean Cam."

"Wow," I laugh. "But you say I need therapy. You got the nerve to tell me what I'm doing wrong, always acting like I can never do anything right, yet you're no better than me. You sorry bastard. You walk around like your shit doesn't stank, like you're a saint who never makes mistakes, yet in a few months your mistake will be born."

"I don't know if that's even my baby."

"You should know, because if you used protection, you wouldn't be in this position, but no, you're so busy trying to find out where I am and all the time I thought it was because you cared, but in actuality you were just trying to make sure we didn't run into each other."

"That's not true."

"Oh, but I have to give you credit, you did a great job at it, because you even had me fooled, but while you were checking on me, you should have been keeping your side chick in check."

"What do you expect from me when you walk around here like you're single? You treat me like I am one of your children and you never take my feelings into consideration. You come in at all times of day and night, wear all this sexy-ass lingerie and there's no telling who you're sleeping with, but now you want to act like I've committed the ultimate crime. I made a mistake."

"Great speech. You almost brought me to tears, but it was actually the bullshit starting to burn my eyes. I've never said I was a saint, because I sin every day, yet I never allow it to affect our home. You get sex whenever, wherever, and however you want it and no matter what I've done outside this home, it has never been brought here, so you can save all that shit for somebody who gives a damn because mine has run completely out. You fucked up and got caught; point blank period."

"So what now?"

"Now, you get the fuck out of my face!"

"But—"

That was all he got out before I threw my glass right at his head.

"I asked you to get out my face. The next time something gets thrown, I won't miss."

# Chapter 12

I put on this sexy jean overall paired with a tight white knit shirt; underneath that showed a little bit of skin, a dark blue blazer and some badass heels that matched my jacket. Then I put on a little bit of makeup, combed my hair and grabbed my clutch bag and headed for the door; leaving Thomas sitting there looking stupid.

I make it to the grand opening of Todd's new restaurant CHLO downtown and it was packed. I gave my keys to the valet as I make my way inside. I go straight for the bar and order a glass of wine when I feel someone's hand grab me.

"Cam?"

Turning around to see who it is; I look right at him. "Todd! Hey, this place is amazing."

"Thanks. You look amazing. Chloe said she didn't know if you were coming."

"I know; I wanted to surprise you guys."

"I am happy you did. She didn't think you would come. Follow me and I will take you where everyone is."

I grab my glass from the bartender and follow Todd through the crowd back to the VIP section.

"Camille!" I hear Chloe scream out. "Oh my God, you're here," she says, with tears in her eyes.

"Oh, don't cry. Why are you crying?" I say, pulling her into a hug.

"I didn't think you would come. I've missed you."

"I've missed you too and I wouldn't have missed this. This place is amazing. You guys have outdone yourself."

"Thank you, but this is Todd's baby. Come on, everyone else is here. Where is Thomas?"

"I left him at home."

"Look who is here," Chloe announces when we make it to the table.

"Cam!" Lyn says shocked, "Wow, you look amazing."

"Thanks, hey everybody."

"Cam, where is my man Thomas?" Paul asks.

"He's at home. I am riding solo tonight. Where are Kerri and Shelby?"

"Kerri is about to pop, so she is sitting this one out and Shelby is sick." Chloe says.

"And here I was thinking we would have an unofficial girl's night." I laugh.

"I can be your girl tonight," Lyn says to me.

"Dinner is served," Todd says, coming to the table followed by a line of servers.

Ray leans over, "Is everything okay?"

"We will talk later," I say, after giving Lyn's ass the evil eye.

After eating and drinking, Todd had an area set aside for a dance floor and the party had officially started. Of course, Ray and I had been out there most of the night and it felt good to hang out with her again.

"I'll be right back; I'm going to the ladies room."

When I walked out the bathroom, I ran into Lyn.

"Hey," she says, looking me over.

"What do you want Lyn?" I ask, looking at her just standing there.

"You are looking great in that jumpsuit."

"What do you want?"

"I was just giving you a compliment."

"Yeah, well thank you. I am heading back to the party."

"Can I have a hug?"

"No. I told you before you need to get some help."

I don't know what is going on with this girl, but let me get out this bathroom before I have to slap the shit out of her.

I stop by the bar for another glass of wine, when I see a young lady from the office.

"Mrs. Shannon, hey."

"Sharon, hey, what are you doing here?"

"My sister is the manager of one of Todd's other restaurants. What about you?"

"Todd's wife is my best friend."

Lyn cleared her throat, which makes me turn around. "Aren't you going to introduce me to your little friend?"

"Excuse you?" I ask, looking at her crazy.

"Mrs. Shannon, it was good seeing you. I will see you on Monday."

"Lyn, what is your problem?"

"Nothing, you were being rude."

"Rude? I didn't know you were still behind me, but that still didn't give you the right to act like I owed you an introduction. You're a friend, not my girlfriend." I walk back to the table to grab my purse. "Ladies and gentlemen, I am going to call it a night. Todd, this place is gorgeous and I have no doubt it will be just as successful as the others," I say, giving him a hug. "Chloe, let's do lunch when I get back from Miami."

"I'd like that. Have a safe trip," she says, standing to give me a hug.

"Ray, call me tomorrow. Good night everybody."

I walk as fast as my legs could carry me getting to valet. I didn't want to take the chance of Lyn following me. I didn't know what was up with her, but I wasn't giving her another opportunity to be alone with me. Something was definitely off.

# Chapter 13

I got up a little earlier than I had planned. The kids were still out, so I decided to surprise Shelby at church this morning. We usually go every Sunday, but I hadn't been in over a month. I don't know where Thomas slept, because I wasn't concerned about that. I showered and got dressed before heading downstairs for a cup of coffee.

"Good morning," Thomas says when I walk in the kitchen. "You headed to church?"

I'm not sure what made him think I would want to have a conversation with him, so I continue making my coffee while he sat at the table looking crazy. I put the top on my travel mug, throw my clutch from last night into my regular purse, grab my keys and walk out.

To keep from walking in church by myself, I stop by Shelby's house to go with her. It was still early, so I knew she would still be home. After ringing the doorbell four times, I was about to leave when Jyema opened the door, out of breath.

"Oh, it's you."

"Hello to you too, is Shelby here?"

"No," she says, about to close the door.

"Wait. What is your problem?"

"Um, I don't have a problem. You asked a question, I answered it; we are done."

"I don't know what your deal is, but I was trying to catch Shelby before she went to church."

"Well you didn't, because she's already gone. Now is there anything else you need?"

"No, but thank you so much for all your help, you've been so kind."

"You're welcome, bitch!"

"What did you call me?"

"I called you a bitch. Isn't that what you are? Or should I have said whore, because any woman who goes after another's woman husband is just that."

"Girl, nobody wants your husband."

"Then what do you call being caught with his dick in your mouth?"

"Giving head, you should try it sometime; it may help you relieve some stress."

"Fuck you!"

"I would let you, but you might like it."

"You hoes kill me; get the hell on before I have to put my hands on you."

"Baby, the only way you can put your hands on me is to undress me, which is what you really want to do, so let me start," I say, unzipping my skirt while walking into the house and closing the door. Letting my skirt hit the floor, I ask, "Is this what you want?" Removing my top, I throw it on top of my skirt as I stand there in my bra and thongs. "Now you can put your hands on me."

"Put your clothes back on and get out. I don't want you."

"Of course you do. You want to see what is so good about Cam that makes your husband's mouth water when he is in my presence, don't you? You're really upset that you didn't find out first, so come on, you can taste her. She doesn't bite."

"I am not going to ask you again," she says, walking over to the door to open it.

I walk right behind her and close it again. Turning her around, I place my back against the door as I grab her hand and place it on my now wet candy box.

"What are you doing? Stop!" Jyema says, trying to snatch her hand away.

"I don't know why you're fighting," I say, placing her hand inside my thong. "You know you want to."

With my hand still on top of hers, I begin to play in candy land. When I felt her relax, I move my hand as she continues to play and when she inserts a finger into me, I smile. I open my legs a little to give her more access to the area she is now enjoying, as she kneels down to remove my panties. Pushing my legs open a little more, her lips slowly find the sweetness I'm sure she's been dreaming about. She takes me in her mouth and I can tell this wasn't her first time pleasing a woman, because this chick had mad skills. Her mouth is so warm and her head fits perfectly between my legs. She had me moaning with sheer pleasure as she inserts two fingers at the right time. I grab her head as I rock into my orgasm.

"Your turn," she says as she walks over to retrieve my clothes from the floor and walk up the stairs.

"With pleasure," I say, locking the door before following her to the guest bedroom.

By the time I make it, she is undressing, so I walk over to her and begin kissing her, tasting my juices that were still on her lips. "How did I taste?"

"Sweet, but you know that already."

"Yeah, but it's always good to be reminded," I said, pushing her on the bed. Starting from her lips, I kiss my way down, taking my time at her round size D breasts that fill my mouth. I pay extra attention to her nipples, because they seem to be her spot. I kiss down her stomach, lingering there for a moment. "Do you squirt?"

"I can, but only with the right person."

"Um, well let's see if I fit into that category," I said, taking her clit into my mouth. Spreading her lips apart, I want all of her as I licked the juices that were flowing. Using my tongue, I slowly slid it up and down as she moans, gripping the covers on the bed.

"Oh God!"

Inserting two fingers into her, I feel her muscles tightening around them as I work to reach her spot.

"Oooh!"

"This must be the spot."

"Don't stop!"

I moved a little to the side as I continue to hit the spot that is making her legs shake.

"Oh my—" she screams, as she begins squirting all over my hand.

Smiling as I slowly move up, I can see her eyes are still closed.

"Are you okay?"

"I cannot believe I just did this. I haven't been with another woman since college."

"Girl, quit lying. The way you eat pussy, you do that on a regular," I say, lingering over her as her hands caress my body.

"I do not. I am happily married and my husband would have a fit if he knew I was doing another woman without him, but he would really go ballistic to find out it was you." She giggles as I kiss her neck while our bodies rub together.

"You may have him fooled, but not I; but I'll play along with you," I tell her as I insert my tongue into her mouth, and she moves her hand back to my box that is still dripping wet.

"You feel so good. Shit!"

"Um, I'm cumming!" I moan out as I suck on her lip. Breathing hard, I roll off her.

"I can see why Brock can't get enough of you."

"Where is Brock?"

"He's out of town on business."

"I thought you guys moved into your own house or are y'all still staying here?"

"No, we have our own house, but Brenae was acting funny this morning and Shelby had to be at church early to help with a Women's Day Breakfast, so she called me to come over. I told her I would bring her to church for the later service after she took a nap."

"That was nice of you."

"Are you still going to church?"

"I was until you had me sinning in my best friend's house."

"Don't act like this was my fault. This was all you."

"Whatever. I guess we both need to go especially after this." I laugh. "What time is it anyway?"

"Ten fifteen."

"I still have time to catch the morning service."

"Or we can have breakfast and you can go with me to the noon service."

"Um, I don't know. You might take advantage of me again." I laugh.

"Whatever. Let me check on Bre and then I'm going to make me something to eat. If you want something, I'll be in the kitchen."

# Chapter 14

I decide to stay and have breakfast and I was glad I did. Being able to talk to someone other than my girls was refreshing, because she didn't have that judgmental tone they normally have in their voice. I did go to church and yes, I repented for my sins. Lord knows I had to.

I decide against joining Shelby and Jyema for lunch and since I had time to kill before picking up Courtney from Lyn's house, I decided to go to the mall. I couldn't even recall the last time I've been able to shop by myself and with the trip coming up; I need a few pieces for the beach.

"Shit," I whisper to myself when I see Dr. Scott coming out of the door I was walking towards.

"Mrs. Shannon, how are you?"

"I am great and the name is Cam."

"Cam, you are looking good. I hope you've thought about the session we have coming up on Tuesday."

"Yeah, I have, but I won't be able to make it. I'm taking the kids to Miami to see my parents."

"When are you leaving?"

"Tuesday," I reply with a bit of an attitude.

"Then why don't you come tomorrow. I don't usually see patients on Mondays, but I will make an exception for you."

"You don't have to do that. If I choose to come next week, I will."

"I don't have to, but I want to. Come by tomorrow at your usual time."

"But—"

"See you then," she said, before walking off.

Bitch!

After being left standing at the entrance of the mall, I finally make my way inside to shop. Usually I don't like to shop, but today it actually felt good. I bought the kids and me some new swimming suits and a few outfits, before I head to Macy's for a new purse and some perfume. As soon as I step inside the store, my phone rings.

I look at it and decide to let it go to voicemail, because I didn't recognize the number. As I start to put the phone in my purse, whoever it was calls repeatedly; again, I let it go to voicemail. If it's important, leave a message.

By the time I make it to the car, I was worn out. I don't think I've ever stayed in the mall that long. Shit! I thought remembering that I had to pick up Courtney. Digging in my purse, I pull out my phone to call her when I see the voicemail notification.

"Mrs. Shannon, my name is Detective Craig Harris with the Memphis Police Department and I need to speak to you regarding an important matter. Please give me a call back at 901-636-3661 as soon as possible."

Memphis Police Department? I thought, as I save the message and call Courtney to tell her I was on my way.

Pulling up outside of Lyn's house, I decide not to go in. After the way she was acting at Todd's restaurant, I didn't need to see her. I grab my phone to call Courtney. After calling three times, she still wasn't answering. Shit! Ringing the doorbell, I wait.

"Hey Mom," Courtney said opening the door.

"Hey little girl, where is your phone?"

"It's on the charger. We are about to eat dinner. Are you coming in?"

"No, I am tired. Get your stuff and let's go."

"Cam, is that you? Come on in, we were about to eat."

"Lyn, hey. I'm not staying. I was just telling this child to get her stuff, because I am tired and ready to get home."

"Okay. I'll be right back. Can you grab my iPad out of the kitchen for me?" Courtney asks, running upstairs.

"Cam, I want to apologize for last night. I had too much to drink, Paul and I have been going through some things and I've missed our friendship. Seeing you the other night, I made an ass of myself. Can you please forgive me?"

"Of course I can, but are you sure you are alright?"

"Yes."

"What is going on with you and Paul? I thought everything was good with y'all."

"I think we've outgrown each other and we are both too stubborn to admit it."

"So what are you going to do? You can't just stay here and be miserable. It will drive you crazy."

"I know but don't worry about me; I will make a decision soon. Anyway, what about you?"

"Well seeing that I found out Thomas has been cheating on me, I've been great."

"Shut the fuck up! Are you serious?"

"As a heart attack."

"How did you find out? And why aren't you pissed?"

"He was arguing with her outside the restaurant we went to yesterday before the party. And she's pregnant."

"Again, why are you not pissed?"

"I am Lyn, you have no idea. I was so mad yesterday that I wanted to run him and her ass over. I mean he has treated me like crap lately and I finally know it was because he was cheating. Now I have this whole judge nomination thing going through my head, along with going to visit my parents; shit, I don't know what to do."

"Wait, judge thing?"

"Yea, I've been nominated to fill Judge Sumner's seat in my district. I thought Shelby would have told you. But, I don't even know if I want to stay married, let alone take this position if I am chosen. I mean, I do my thing Lyn, but I've never bought it to our home; to have Thomas cheating on me is one thing, but having a baby on the way is something totally different."

"Daddy's having another baby?"

# Chapter 15

"Shit! You weren't supposed to hear that."

"Mom, you said Dad has been cheating on you and now has a baby on the way. Please tell me that's not true."

"I can't because it is."

"How long have you known?" she asks, starting to cry.

"I just found out yesterday."

"I hope you beat his ass."

"No," I say laughing, "and we will talk about this later with your dad. You can ask him all the questions you want. Now, stop crying. Are you ready?"

"Yes, but I forgot my charger. Hold on," she says, running back upstairs again.

"Shit! Shit! I didn't mean for her to hear me."

"She was going to find out anyway. So, what are you going to do now?"

"I honestly don't know Lyn. Do you know he had the nerve to say he cheated, because I was never at home?"

"That's a lame-ass excuse that all men use. Do you even know the chick?"

"Yes, we've been with her together a few times."

"Hold up, is she the one you used for his birthday a few years back?"

"Yes."

"That sorry bastard. He couldn't find anyone else?"

"Obviously not. I guess you can say I made it easy, because I brought his mistress home."

"Are you serious? You were giving him every man's fantasy—not permission to impregnate someone else. You need to get a grip. This isn't the Cam I know, who would have torn the restaurant up with his ass."

"I know—"

"Stop saying I know. What are you going to do?" she asked, sitting down in front of me.

"That I don't know. If I am chosen to fill this position, how would it look if I am going through a divorce?"

"You'd look like everyone else who has gone through a divorce. Cam, the last thing you want is an unhappy home, trust me, I know. If you choose to stay with Thomas, stay because you want to and not because you're worried about what everyone else will say or because it's the right thing to do. And please don't say I know."

"Yes ma'am," I say smiling, when I pull my phone from my jacket.

"Thomas?"

"No, Judge Alton. Crap, I forgot I was supposed to meet him for dinner tonight to discuss all this judge crap."

"Go ahead. Leave Courtney here until you come back."

"You sure?"

"Yeah. Go on. I'll tell her."

"Thanks. I won't be long." I tell her as I text Charles to let him know I am on my way.

"And Cam?"

"Yes Lyn."

"Don't make a decision about your future based on this mess. You can be a great judge, married or divorced."

I walk back over to give her a hug. "Thank you."

"You're welcome. Now go!"

\*\*\*

I make it to the hotel Charles and I normally meet. When he wasn't at the bar, I called him.

"Hey, where are you?"

"Room 324," he says, before hanging up as I walk to the elevators.

"Hey, you're looking good," he says, pulling me into the room.

"I thought we were having dinner."

"I am," he says, pulling my jacket off. "Have you decided to run in the election?"

"Is that why you called me over, because I thought you were hungry?"

"Oh, I am definitely hungry, I was just making conversation."

"Talk later," I say, removing my shirt and bra.

"You can take everything off, but leave the shoes on."

"Now what?" I ask, smiling after getting undressed.

"Now bring your ass over here."

"You're finally taking charge, I like that."

"Good," he says, slapping me on my butt before kissing the same spot. "Get on your knees."

I did as he says, as he continues to kiss all over my butt, before spreading my cheeks to lick. When I feel his fingers go there, I move.

"No sir! The back door is a privilege you've yet to earn."

"Really? We will see," he says as he continues to lick me from behind. As I began to play with my clit, he inserts a finger into me.

"Hmm," I say, pushing back onto his finger.

"You're so wet."

I smiled and rolled over as I continued playing with myself, while watching him watch me. He stood there as I licked my fingers before sliding two of them back into me. I knew exactly were my spot was and I could make myself squirt, so I decided to give him a show.

"Damn girl, you've been holding back on me, but I like it," he said, climbing on top of me.

"Condom!" I remind him as he jumps off the bed to get one. He puts it on as he climbs back on top of me.

Grabbing his cock, I push him into me as I wrap my legs around his back.

He pulls my hands over my head and holds them there as he pounds into me just the way I like.

"You feel so good!" he moans in my ear.

"Show me."

He did just that as he gives me orgasm after orgasm. Flipping me over, he enters me and it feels damn good. Slapping my ass as he rides me hard from behind, I feel another orgasm coming. "Right there, yes, right there!"

"Is that your spot? Right here?"

"Yes, yes! I'm cumming," I scream.

Oh shit," he grunts before collapsing on my back. "Damn girl, you still amaze me."

"Do I?" I laugh, pushing him off me. "I see you've been taking notes because your sex game is getting much better."

"I'm a great learner."

"Alright, Mr. Great Learner. Don't get in trouble with your wife trying to show off all these new moves."

"Don't worry. She loves them. She actually wants me to thank you."

"Then I'm doing my job." I laugh.

"You know it. I don't know what you're trying to do to me."

"I don't know what you're talking about," I said, kicking my shoes off before pulling the cover over me.

"Wait, what's up with you? You never lay down next to me."

"Hell, I don't know. I have a lot on my mind."

"You want to talk about it? Is it the election?" he said, pulling me next to him.

"Yes and the fact that my husband has been cheating and has a baby on the way."

"Wow."

73

"I know, but how can I feel bad about him cheating when I'm cheating?"

"That's a good question, but have you ever been pregnant by someone else?"

"Hell no!"

"Exactly.

"But Charles, this shit gets real when it's done to you. If I wasn't thinking about running in this election, I would have whooped Thomas's ass and called it a day, but with everything hanging over my head—"

"Look, you do what you have to do. Yes, having a family is the first thing people look at, but you won't be the first person to get divorced and you surely won't be the last. Your career will speak for itself."

"Yeah, but it's just a lot to think about. I'm going to see my dad this week to talk to him about all of this before I make a decision."

"Is your dad an attorney?"

"He was, but he's a judge now; my mom is an attorney."

"Now, I see where you get it from. What do you think your dad will say?"

# Chapter 16

Before I could answer, I hear my phone ringing in my purse. I got up to get it, thinking it was probably Courtney, but it was the same number who called me earlier, so I decide to answer.

"This is Camille Shannon."

"Mrs. Shannon, this is detective Craig Harris from the Memphis Police Department. There is a matter that I need to speak to you about."

"Okay," I said, walking back over to the bed. "I'm listening."

"Can you come down to the station?"

"Not until you tell me what this is about."

"We got a report that you assaulted a young lady outside a restaurant a few nights ago."

"What?" I laugh. "Are you serious?"

"Very serious? Can you come and speak to me now?"

"Do you have a warrant?"

"Mrs. Shannon, I know these charges are bogus, but I still need to talk to you in person."

"Fine, I'll be there in thirty minutes."

"What was that about?"

"According to Detective Harris, a young lady filed a report saying that I assaulted her the other night at a restaurant."

"What lady?"

"The only one I can think of is the chick Thomas has been seeing."

"Did you?"

"Hell no, but now I wish I had."

"So what did he say? Is there a warrant?"

"No, but he wants me to come and talk to him."

"I'm going with you."

***

"Mrs. Shannon, I presume."

"That's me and this is my attorney Charles Alton."

"You didn't have to bring an attorney because you are not under arrest."

"I know but I'd rather be safe than sorry."

"That's cool. Follow me," he said, leading me into an interrogation room.

"Can you tell me what's going on?"

"We received a report that you physically assaulted a young lady outside Prive' Restaurant on Riverdale Road."

"And let me guess. The person making the report was Michelle Craft."

"Yes. Can you tell me what happened?"

"I walked outside the restaurant to find her and my husband arguing. When I asked what was going on she told me that she was pregnant by my husband."

"And what did you do?"

"I cussed his ass out and left him standing there with her."

"How do you know Ms. Craft?"

"I met her when I hired her to do a threesome with me and my husband for his birthday a few years back."

"No shit! Damn, my bad," he laughs. "I didn't think women actually did that. I'm sorry. Did you see her after that?"

"Yea, we've been together a few times with her after that."

"Did you ever suspect your husband to be cheating?"

"No."

"So you weren't upset enough to physically assault her?"

"Detective Harris, the only thing that saved me from slapping the taste out of that chick's mouth and beating my husband's ass the other night was time."

"What do you mean?"

"My client has been nominated to fill a vacant judge seat in her district."

"And I can't risk this kind of shit being on my record."

"Look, Mrs. Shannon; I don't know what is going on in your personal life, but I can tell you that anyone that will go through filing a false police report is crazy, I suggest you watch yourself."

"Will there be any charges filed?"

"No, because I got the surveillance tapes right before you got here and found out that she is a liar. We will be filing charges on her for filing a false report. Since you were already on the way, I wanted to give you a heads up."

"Thank you, detective. Please let me know if there is anything else I can do."

When I made it to Charles's car, I was fuming. "I can't believe this. This hoe had the nerve to try and file charges on me and she's been sleeping with my husband."

"I know baby, but calm down."

"I've got to be dreaming. This can't be possibly happening," I say, laughing and putting my head back on the seat.

"It will be alright, just calm down. Do you want to go back to the hotel and have a drink?"

"No," I say blowing out a breath. "I need to get my car though, because I told Courtney I would pick her up from Lyn's house."

"Are you sure you are okay to drive?"

"I am. Don't worry, but thank you for coming with me. I am glad you were there."

"Anytime," he said, bending over to kiss me. "You know I have your back."

\*\*\*

When I finally make it home from picking up Courtney, it was late. TJ was in his room asleep and Thomas was in the den. I wait until Courtney went upstairs before I go in to choke the shit out of him. He was asleep on the couch, so I kick him harder than I had too.

"Damn Cam, what's up?'

"Your bitch, that's what's up."

"What are you talking about?" he asks, sitting up.

"I just came from the police station."

"The police station? For what?"

"Because your baby momma said that I assaulted her."

"Are you freaking kidding me? Oh my God, Cam, I am so sorry."

"Why in the fuck would I make this shit up?"

"What happened? Why didn't you call me?"

"Nothing, because they knew the skank was lying, but it still doesn't excuse the fact that she would lie about something that could ruin my life and my career."

"You are right and I am sorry. This shit is my fault, because I never should have slept with her."

"You're right, but you need to fix this shit by the time the kids and I come back from Miami or find somewhere else to stay. The only reason I haven't snapped on your ass is because I might get chosen for the bench; otherwise, I would have clicked the fuck off!"

"I know and—"

"No, you don't know, but you'll find out. Oh and your daughter knows."

"What do you mean?"

"What exactly I said. Your daughter knows that you cheated and that you have a baby on the way with someone other than your wife. So, yeah; good luck with that."

# Chapter 17

Good morning Mrs. Shannon, are you ready for the meeting with the new client?"

"Yes I am Mr. Townsend. Come in and have a seat."

"Have you given any consideration to what we discussed last week?"

"I have and here is the questionnaire back. I am still in shock just to be nominated. How does the process actually work?"

"Well, when there is a vacancy; the Judicial Nominating Committee notifies the public of the vacancy and nominations are made of qualified attorneys. Once the nominations are done, the names are submitted to the Judicial Nominating Committee by way of these questionnaires, they choose three nominees who they then submit via a letter to the governor, who makes his pick."

"Wow. And because the election was just in November, if I am chosen; I will fill the seat until the next election?"

"Yes."

"Okay."

"Camille, you are already prepared for this. You've been prepared. You've worked hard for this and if I didn't think you were ready, I wouldn't have put you in the position."

"Mr. Thompson, I am not worried about doing the job. My biggest fear is being picked apart by the media if I am chosen."

"You let me deal with that. I will handle all of that. You go on and visit that old fart of a father and tell him he still owes me a bottle of scotch."

"Yes, sir. Thank you Mr. Townsend."

As soon as he left, Stephanie buzzed to say that Lyn was here. Lyn? I thought to myself.

"Hey Lyn, what are you doing here?"

"Am I interrupting you, I can always come back?"

"No girl, you're good, come on in. You want something to drink, coffee or water?" I ask, refilling my coffee.

"Yeah, I'll take some coffee. Dang, I didn't know you had all this in your office," she says, admiring the bar.

"That's right; you hadn't been here since we moved. Yeah, it's one of the perks of being partner. I love this office so much better than the old one, because it has everything I need if I have to work late or even sleep here."

"I know, hell; this bathroom is almost as big as mine at home."

"I work hard enough for it," I say, laughing as I hand her a cup of coffee before sitting on the couch. "Now, tell me what brings you here."

"I just wanted to stop through and check on you after our conversation last night to make sure you were alright," she says, looking at me strange.

"Are you sure that's all? You look like there is something bothering you."

"Do you ever think about the relationship you and I shared?" she blurts out.

I almost choke on my coffee. "Lyn, don't start this shit again. After the conversation last night, I thought we were past this."

"I've just been thinking about it lately and when you showed up last night, it made me wonder if you ever think about it sometimes."

"Lyn, be for real. You know how that ended and if I think about it, it'll take me back to that one night that almost cost me my life."

"So, you never think about the sex we used to have?"

"Okay Lyn, what's up? For real, where is this shit coming from all of a sudden?"

"It's like I said. I've just been thinking about it. I'm bored with Paul and we don't have the girl's night like we used to, so I have a lot of time to think."

"Well stop!" I say, getting up to walk over to the bar. "That was the past; it was a mistake we made and it's over and done with. May I suggest you get a hobby, a sex toy, spice up your sex life with Paul or get a boyfriend or shit, a girlfriend?"

"But I want you."

"Um, what the hell? Are you listening to yourself? Do you not recall all the hell that caused us, the both of us, the last time?"

"I know, but I need you, I really need you."

"Stop saying that!" I say, getting pissed. "I really hope this is a bad joke and you're not serious, because we can never go back there. What happened between us was years ago, and we made it past it with our friendship and marriages intact, and I'm not willing to risk either of those again. We are friends, Lyn, best friends and that's it. And if you can't get pass these thoughts you're having, we may need to rethink some things."

"Was I that bad that you'll never look at me like that again?"

"I think it's time for you to go."

"So that's it? You're not going to even take my feelings into consideration?"

"Lyn, listen to yourself. Please stop this! I see where you're headed, because it is the same path I took and you know for yourself that it doesn't end well. For the sake of our friendship, please drop this. May I please suggest you talk to someone and get some professional help, please?"

"So now you're saying I'm crazy?" she says, getting up.

"You sure in hell sound like it. I am not interested in a relationship with you, yet here you are at my job, talking all out your head from a conversation we had last night as friends. Are you on something?"

"Fuck this! I know you still have feelings for me. You just don't want to act on them right now, but it's cool."

"Lyn, listen for the sake of our friendship; please get some help. There is nothing between us and there will be nothing between us, and if you can't understand that, then I don't know if we can continue to be friends."

She starts to cry. "I am so sorry Cam. You are right. I don't know what made me come here. I've been going through some things with Paul and I haven't dealt with them the right way, but I will. Please forgive me."

"Only if you promise to get some help."

"I will, I promise. I'm going to let you go."

"Wait, let me give you the number to my therapist," I say, as Stephanie buzzes.

"Cam, Mrs. Walker is on line one for you."

Before I could stop Lyn, she was gone out the door.

"Thanks Stephanie," I say, still confused by the entire conversation with Lyn.

"Mrs. Walker, how can I help you?"

"Good morning, I was calling to see if your investigator has found anything about my company? I have a meeting with the board next week and they are asking why I fired our other legal firm. I am so sick of going toe-to-toe with these assholes," she says, letting out a breath.

I laugh.

"I apologize. I didn't mean to say all of that, but since I've been handed this company, all I've been getting is flak from the men who thought another man should be the head."

"You don't have to apologize. I totally get your frustration. I am actually meeting with my investigator this afternoon and I will give you call afterwards, but look, don't let them see you sweat. You can vent to me, but in front of them, keep it together. They are waiting for you to have a woman moment."

"Thanks Mrs. Shannon. I really appreciate everything you're doing. Oh, did you receive the invitation to the party?"

"You are welcome; yes I did and I will be there."

"Thanks again. I know I am in capable hands and I am sorry to bother you. I look forward to hearing from you."

# Chapter 18

"Hey Raul, come in."

"Hey Cam. I finished my investigation on Donnington and Associates and everything checked out. All of the audits have cleared from a financial point of view and all of the background checks are in good standing."

"That's interesting. Mr. Donnington seemed to have had all of his shit in order, huh?"

"Yes, he did. The only thing that wasn't legitimate was the other law firm they had. They were charging them an extremely high rate and this company in Miami would have sunk them had they purchased that company."

"I know and that makes me wonder why Mr. Donnington even got involved with them in the first place. I am glad Mrs. Walker followed her instinct and hired us. Thank you Raul."

"You're welcome. Is there anything else you need from me?"

"Yeah. Can you look into something for me off the record?"

"Sure."

"I need you to look into one of my best friends, Lynesha Williams. She owns the boutique over on Main Street called Glam

Street. I will send you some information on her to get you started."

"What's going on with her?"

"I don't know but she has been acting weird, almost stalkerish type shit and I don't need this right now."

"I'm on it."

"Thanks Raul. Call me with whatever you find, it doesn't matter what time."

I decide to call Monica to let her know the good news about the company. She wasn't available, so I left her a message and I also sent her an email. I also decide to call Paul. He had been on my mind especially with everything going on with Lyn lately.

"Cam, what's up?" Paul answers.

"Hey Paul, there's something I need to talk to you about, you got a minute?"

"Sure."

"Is everything okay with Lyn?"

"Your guess is as good as mine. I don't know. Lately she has been acting off and I don't know how to explain it. Why, what happened?"

"She has been popping up in different places where I am and uh—"

"What Cam?"

"Paul, she's been talking about wanting a relationship with me again. I don't know where this is coming from and it's getting kind of weird and scary."

"Damn." He laughs. "I knew she was acting different, but I didn't expect this. I just thought she was going through a midlife crisis or something with Kelsey being gone, but now I see that she is spiraling out of control."

"I am worried about her. I've tried to talk her into getting some help, but she won't hear of it. She starts crying, begs for forgiveness, and acts like she is changing, but then she goes right back to the same crazy attitude. I know where this is heading Paul and it's not going to end well."

"But what can I do? She won't listen to me. Hell, I barely see her most days. I've been staying at a hotel. Even Kelsey is concerned."

"I don't know. I am going to reach out to the girls again when I get back from Miami. Maybe we can stage an intervention or something."

"Okay. Please let me know, because I am willing to help but she will have to want to do it for herself too."

"I know; I will, and Paul, if there is anything I can do, please don't hesitate to call."

I stay at the office a little while longer. I finish working on a few things that I need to get done before I go out of town this week and I wasn't in a hurry to get home to argue with Thomas. As soon as I get ready to call it a night, I get a text from Terrance.

"Come and put me to sleep."

"On my way!" I reply back while grabbing my jacket and purse.

I make it to Terrance's apartment downtown, which wasn't far from my office. He was waiting for me at the door. I leave my computer bag in the front seat and grab my purse and jacket.

He grabs my hand and pulls me over the threshold as he pushes the door closed, locking it. I place my jacket and purse on the nearest chair as he grabs me, pushing me against the wall. Pinning my hands over my head, he inserts his tongue into my mouth as his hand pulls my shirt out of my skirt. Releasing one of my breasts from my bra, he takes it into his mouth as I moan the pleasure of everything he is doing. He releases my hand and I quickly move to pull my shirt off. I then unzip my skirt and allow it to fall to the floor. He turns me around and kisses down the middle of my back. Spreading my legs, he begins to kiss my butt cheeks. Placing my hands on the wall, I push out a little, giving him more access to where he needs to be. He buries his face in between my legs as he licks me from behind.

"Hmmm..." I moan as he spreads my legs wider and licks harder. "Oooh, don't stop!"

He rips my thongs off as he opens my ass, burying his head down to reach my clit from behind, causing me to scream out. I know I left scratch marks on the wall as he sucks me for dear life.

"Oh God!"

He slides up and steps back long enough to put on a condom that was on the sofa table not far from us. He turns back and grabs my waist, pulling me to him before entering me without a word. I put my hands on the wall and...

"Don't stop!"

Still he says nothing. Which doesn't bother me, because I am feeling every inch of him and...

"Why did you stop?"

"Is that your car alarm?"

"What?"

He completely stops and goes over to the window to hear my car alarm going off. "Babe, your window is shattered."

"Are you serious?" I ask, putting my skirt back on and trying to find my shirt while Terrance went to get dressed.

"Don't go out until I come back."

# Chapter 19

We finally make it downstairs; after turning the alarm off, I notice a note on the driver's side seat.

"Wow," I laugh!

"What does it say?" Terrance asks.

I hand him the note and he reads it aloud. "Karma is a bitch, bitch!" "Damn babe, who would do this?"

"Probably Thomas' baby momma."

"Wait, say what now? Your husband has a baby momma?"

"Yep and it was probably her trifling ass that did this."

"You need to call the police."

"No, I don't need that drama. I will deal with that when I get home. Can you drop me off at home?"

"What about your car?"

"I'll come back in the morning and get the window repaired. I don't feel like dealing with this shit tonight."

"Are you sure you want me to drive you home?"

"You scared?"

"No, let me grab my keys and wallet."

I walk around to the passenger side to grab my computer bag from the seat. I am glad the dumb heifer didn't have sense enough to take it.

\*\*\*

"Where have you been?" Thomas asks when I got home.

"Who are you talking to?"

"I don't want to argue with you, I—"

"Then don't question me. You lost that privilege when you got your side piece pregnant."

"Cam, please don't start that tonight. I know I fucked up, but I don't want to go there with you tonight."

"Then get the fuck out my face."

"Why do you have to be so mean? I told you that I am sorry, what else do you want from me?"

"Man dude, man up and stop whining. You were man enough to pump sperm into a chick that wasn't your wife, without a condom might I add, and get her pregnant; then you ought to be man enough to deal with a pissed off wife!"

"I'm sorry Camille."

"Stop apologizing to me. Did you find out why she tried to file charges on me?"

"She said she didn't."

"Oh, and you believe her? Well, I guess the police department would make up that lie just to see my face."

"I don't know. I am only telling you what she told me."

"Well, I guess she's going to tell you she didn't bust the window out my car tonight either, huh?"

"She did what? Where? Did you see her do it?"

"I didn't have to see her do it. She left a note saying, 'Karma is a bitch, bitch.' Who else would have a reason to bust my fucking window out?"

"I'll take care of your window. Where are your keys?"

"I don't need you to take care of my keys and my car isn't here. I left it at work. I had a coworker to bring me home. I'll take care of it in the morning."

"A coworker bought you home? Why didn't you call your husband?"

"Because I didn't want to, do you have any more questions?"

"Dammit Camille, I'm trying to apologize for my mistakes. I am trying to make it up to you!"

"Good for you," I say, before slamming the bedroom door.

# Chapter 20

Therapy Session

"Mrs. Shannon, I am glad you could make it."

"My name is Cam."

"Well Cam—"

"Look, can we get this over with? I have a trip to pack for."

"I am sure I've told you before that the attitude doesn't hold up within these walls, so drop it. Why don't you start by telling me about yourself?"

"What do you want to know?"

"Everything."

"My name is Camille Janae Shannon. I am thirty-seven years old with two children and I am a kick-ass partner at my law firm. I didn't come from an abusive home and I don't have daddy issues. I love the taste of dick and occasionally dabble in pussy. I love to dress, although I don't like to shop. I haven't seen my parents in years, but I'm going to visit them this week. Oh, I've been nominated to fill the seat of a judge who had to step down in my district." I paused. "Um, that's about it."

"Are you married?"

"What's today?" I laugh. "Yes, I'm married."

"But?"

"But what? You asked and I told you."

"You didn't mention that when I asked you to tell me about yourself."

"I'm aware."

"Why is that?"

"Oh, because I'm married to a no-good motherfucker who cheated with someone, and now has a baby on the way."

"How does that make you feel?"

"Seriously?"

"I am very serious. How does it make you feel to know your husband would sleep with another woman behind your back, and now has a baby on the way?"

"It makes me feel like I am married to a no-good motherfucker who cheated with someone and now she's pregnant with his child."

"Cam, I can't help you if you won't be honest with me."

"I don't need your help."

"Then why do you have an attitude with me?"

"Because you keep asking me all these crazy ass questions."

"Fine, then tell me why you think Dr. Nelson would refer you to me?"

"Why don't you ask him? Our therapy sessions were over a long time ago and the only reason I kept seeing him was because he licks my—"

"I get the point' however, if you were expecting me to be shocked by that, I'm not, because you use sex as a means of getting out of situations that make you uncomfortable."

"I use sex as a means of pleasing me."

"Then why get married?"

"Why not?"

"Why get married, only to cheat on your husband?"

"I didn't get married to cheat. I got married because I loved my husband, but then life happened and I got bored."

"So why not take up a hobby, or talk to your husband about spicing up your sex life?"

"I did talk to him, but he didn't want to do anything else. Hell, I gave him a threesome for his birthday and look where that got us. That motherfucker sleeps with her behind my back and now she's pregnant. Of all the women to sleep with, he picks her."

"Do you blame yourself?"

"Hell no. Why would I blame myself for the mistake he made? I didn't tell him to sleep with her behind my back and not use protection."

"Didn't you bring her into your lives?"

"Yes, I brought her into our lives as in the both of us."

"But you had to know there would be consequences, right?"

"Yeah, that both of us would be satisfied."

"Both or just you? Be real Cam, for once."

"I am being real. I didn't have to bring another woman into our bed to be satisfied. If I want another woman, I can have that. I brought her into our lives, because it's what he always wanted as a fantasy. Look, I don't know what you want to hear, but I always keep it real. I love sex; period and I don't blame myself for him falling into that trap. Hell, any man would love to have a wife like me that is willing to give him every sex fantasy he dreams of, but not that bald head motherfucker."

"Again, I have to ask; why did you get married?"

"It was the right thing to do."

"Do you love your husband?"

"Yes, but I'm not in love with him and before you ask why I stay, I don't know. I guess because it's the right thing to do. Being a partner in a firm that prides itself on family, what else am I supposed to do?"

"You're supposed to be happy and from the attitude you have now, you are still in love with your husband."

"I am happy. Don't I look like it? I have a husband, children who are good, a nice home and cars, a job that I love and great friends. What is there to be unhappy about?"

"Your husband choosing someone else beside you. See, you like to dish out things, but you can't accept it when it's given back to you and now that your husband has chosen someone else, you're upset about it."

I start laughing. "You don't know me."

"When will you stop running Cam?"

"What makes you think I'm running? Girl, don't you see the shoes I have on? There's no way I can run in these."

"See, this is exactly what I mean. You keep hiding behind this wall you've put up."

"And let me guess, you think I use sex as an outlet."

"The first step is admitting it."

97

"I don't have anything to hide. I love sex and I won't be shy about that. Plus, who am I hurting?"

"Yourself. You're hurting yourself, because although you look together on the outside, you are a complete mess on the inside. You want everybody to think you're this chick who has it all, but you're slowly dying on the inside. Yes, you can walk in those five-inch heels, wear the nice suit that conforms to your shape, drive the expensive car, stay in the big house, work at your dream job and put up the smokescreen for your coworkers and friends, but it won't last long."

"Are we done?"

"Yes, for now. I'll see you at the same time next week. Have a safe trip and call me if you need me."

"You'll be the first on my list. Have a great night, Doc."

\*\*\*

"Hey, y'all all packed? We have an early flight in the morning."

"Yes ma'am. Our bags are packed and by the door." TJ said, sounding so excited.

"Good. Where is your sister?"

"She's in her room. She's had an attitude all day."

"Okay. I'll check on her," I said, kissing him goodnight.

"Hey, you okay?" I ask, walking into Courtney's room.

"Yeah, why do you ask?" she replies, removing her headphones.

"Your brother said you've had an attitude all day. What's up?"

"Nothing, I'm just ready for this vacation."

"Are you sure? You know you can talk to me, right?"

"I know, but I'm fine Mom."

"If you say so, but I am here for you. Get some sleep, because we have an early flight."

"I know. Goodnight."

I knew this thing with her dad was bothering her, but I was not going to push the issue. When she is ready to talk to me, she will. I just hate they have to deal with this. That motherfucker! I mumble when I walk into the bedroom to find Thomas sitting on the bed.

"I am not in the mood for your shit tonight, Thomas."

"Hello to you too. I didn't come in here to start anything with you."

"Then what do you want?"

"I want you to talk to me. I miss you, I miss us."

I laugh. "Dude look, I have to finish packing."

"Why are you laughing? I am serious Cam. I miss us."

"I'm laughing, because you've got to be joking. You sleep with Chelle behind my back, after I allow her to be in the bed with us whenever you ask. Oh, but get this, not only did you sleep with her behind my back, but you get her pregnant. Oh, oh; but then to add insult to injury, your hoe files assault charges against me and busts the window out my car. Are you serious?"

"I know but I am so sorry. I never meant for any of this to happen. Baby, you've got to believe me," he said, walking over to me.

"Don't."

"Baby, please," he says, pushing me against the wall while kissing my neck. "Please, I need you." Continuing to kiss my breast, I let out a slight sigh as he moves to the other breast and takes my nipple into his mouth.

"I miss you. I'm so sorry," he said, as I push him further down. Leaning against the wall, I put one leg over his shoulder while his mouth finds my mound of caramel.

"Ooh, use more tongue; yes, yes, like that." I moan while grabbing the back of his head. "Don't stop! Shit!" I scream out as he continues to suck on my clit. He's sucking so good that my other leg is beginning to shake. "Oh God, I'm cumming!"

"Damn girl," he says, standing up to unzip his pants.

"Damn boy, you've always been great with your tongue," I tell him as I push him back against the wall, walking past him to the bathroom. "Close the door on your way out."

# Chapter 21

"Miami Life"

"Sly, they're here!" I hear my mother yell as we pull into the driveway.

"Grandma!" the kids scream as they jump out the car.

"My babies, I've missed you all so much."

"We missed you too. Where's Grandpa?"

"Here I am," my dad, Sylvester Holden said, walking down the steps.

"Grandpa!"

"Where is your mom?"

"Here I am. Hey Dad, I've missed you," I say, running into his arms.

"Hey baby girl. I've missed you too. Maybe you ought to think about visiting more."

"Sylvester, don't start with my baby, she just got here," My momma said, slapping my dad's arm. "Come and give your momma a hug."

"Hey Mom, wow, you are looking good."

"I know, right?" she says, turning around.

"Come on in the house. Where are your bags?" my dad asks.

"They're in the trunk, let me help you."

"No, I got it. Go on inside. Your mom has lunch prepared."

"I am so glad you're home. How have you been? Your dad told me that you've been nominated to fill an empty seat in your district. I'm so proud of you."

"Thanks, but I haven't even been chosen yet."

"Girl, you are the best woman for the job. You got this. Why do you doubt it?"

"I don't know Mom, it's a big decision."

"Yes and it's one that I know you've been working hard for."

"I have, but if I am chosen, I don't want my entire life scrutinized by the media."

"Listen, don't let the fear of that stop you from claiming this position, Camille."

"My daughter is afraid of something?" my dad asks, coming into the kitchen. "What are you so scared of?

"I don't know Dad."

"Spill it, Camille."

"I'm telling you the truth Dad. I don't know what's holding me back, I'm just scared."

"What is Thomas saying?"

"Camille?"

"I really don't care what Thomas has to say at this point, because I don't know if he and I will be married much longer."

"What did that motherfucker do?"

"Sylvester!"

"What Sylvia? I'm just asking a question."

"He cheated."

"Awl, baby girl, you can get through that," my dad said, waving his hand.

"And he has a baby on the way."

"You can work through that too," my mom said, taking something out of the oven.

"And it's with a girl that I allowed to come into our bed."

"Awl, hell no!" They both said together.

"Shit! I need a drink," my dad says, shaking his head.

"I'll fix it because we all need one," I tell them, walking over to the bar. "You still drink Crown and Coke?" I ask my dad.

"No, just the new apple Crown. It's on the bar. Now, let me get this straight. You invited a woman into your bed, and not only did Thomas cheat on you with this same woman, but she's now pregnant?"

"Yep," I said, talking a big gulp of the Crown. "This is good."

"Is this why you're afraid to accept the nomination? You think this will get out?"

"It's not just that. It's the fact of being in the public's eye."

"But you're already in the public's eye. Every time you step foot inside a courtroom, you're in the public eye. So what aren't you telling us?"

"Nothing Mom, that's it."

"Lil girl, let me tell you this. No human being living or dead is perfect. Hell, we all make mistakes, but don't allow your personal life to stop you from being called Judge Camille Shannon; let your work speak for you. Your dad and I aren't perfect by a long shot, and we stay in the public's eye."

"But how was it for you when Dad ran the first time?"

"It was hard, but it was something that he's always wanted and I knew that before we got married, so I prepared myself for it. Will there be some hard stuff to deal with? Yes, but it's all a part of the job," my mom answered.

"Listen baby, becoming a judge and staying a judge is hard, but if it's something you want to do, then do it. I know that you are one hell of an attorney, because you've placed your mark in a field that has been male dominated for as long as it's been around. Stop letting fear beat you at the game you've set the rules for."

"But what if I decide to get a divorce?"

"Will it change your work ethic? Will it remove everything you've learned about the law? Would it make you less of an attorney? Will it make you less than a judge?"

"No but—"

"But what? Whatever you decide to do in your personal life is just that. Yes, the media will run with it, but so what? Every time they run something negative, give them something positive," my dad answers.

"I should come home more often."

"Yes you should. Now, go and wash your hands so we can eat. I invited some family and friends to come over later. You know it's not often our baby is home."

"Tonight? But we just got here," I say, pouting.

"And you will just be ready for the party. Now wash up and get the kids."

"Yes ma'am!"

# Chapter 22

"Camille, are you ready?" my mom yells for the fiftieth time. "People will be here soon."

"Yes Mom!" I yell back. "Give me five minutes and I'll be down."

"Mom, why is Grandma freaking out about this party?" Courtney asks, coming into my room.

"She's just excited about us being here, that's all."

"Dang, then we've definitely got to start coming here more often."

"Alright lil girl, watch your mouth. Let's get downstairs before your grandma comes up here swinging."

I make it downstairs to see my mom talking to the chef for tonight.

"I thought you said it was going to be a small get-together," I say, walking into the kitchen.

"It is."

"Then why did you bring in a chef?"

"Who, Jules? He's been our chef for the last three years. You would know that if you came home more often."

"Okay, okay; I know and I am going to work on that. I promise."

"Oh, before I forget; one of my clients is having a book signing Friday night and I want you to go with me."

"Which client?"

"Johnie Jay. His third book released two weeks ago and it's already on the New York Times Best Sellers list."

"When did you start representing authors?"

"Um, I am an entertainment lawyer, remember? And—"

"If I came home more often, I know Mom." I finish her sentence as I heard my Aunt Sara's voice. "Auntie!"

"There's my baby. Look at you looking like you looking," she, spinning me around. "Memphis has been good to you I see. All that southern cooking is going right to your booty."

"I know right, and it looks good doesn't it?" I laugh, giving her a hug.

"Only you would think so," says my cousin Reese, Aunt Sara's daughter.

"Hey to you too, Reese." I say. She and I have never gotten along. She has never liked me and I return the favor.

"Oh hush up Reese; you're just jealous because your skinny ass could use ten more pounds." Aunt Sara says.

"Ten pounds? Are you crazy? I'll never be bigger than a size four," she says as this fine ass cream-colored dude walks up next to her.

"We all know, which is why you've yet to give me a baby," he says, putting one hand around her waist. "Hey, I'm Noah, Reese's husband. You must be her cousin Camille, the attorney?"

"Cam and yes I am. It's nice to meet you."

"Likewise and if you don't mind I'd like to ask you some questions about the bar exam, later."

"Okay, sure. Are you studying to take it?"

"Yes, in two months."

"Congratulations. I'd be happy to answer any questions you have."

"I'd bet you are," Reese says under her breath.

"Did you say something Reese?" I step back and ask.

"Well if it isn't Camille Holden."

I turn to see whom it is calling me by my maiden name, and I almost burst out laughing when I see the face of my old high school sweetheart. "James?"

"Yeah, you don't recognize me? I know I've gotten older, but dang."

"With all of this," I say rubbing his stomach, "I almost didn't recognize you."

"That's what eating good does for you, but I see that you haven't aged a bit."

"And we see that you need glasses," Reese says, before walking out the room.

"It's good to see you James," I say, while rolling my eyes in Reese's direction. "What have you been up to?" I ask, walking to the back patio.

"From the looks of it, it looks like I should have been up to Memphis. Damn girl, you are fine."

"Okay, down boy. I'm sure you are married."

"Yeah, but what's that got to do with anything? I know you haven't forgotten how I used to lay it down."

"Boy please! We were in high school. A lot has changed since then."

"I'm sure the taste of that sweet pussy hasn't changed."

"Wow, I see you haven't changed a bit. Goodnight James."

Fat pervert!

# Chapter 23

"Did you say something?" Noah asks, startling me.

"Oh my God, you scared the crap out of me."

"I'm sorry. I heard you say something, so I thought you were talking to me."

"No, I was talking about James, but I didn't realize I had said it out loud," I say, laughing. "Do you want a drink?"

"Sure, what are you having?"

"A glass of wine."

"No thanks to the wine, but I'd take a beer."

"I'll be right back." Walking over to the bar to get our drinks, I couldn't help but wonder what in the hell Noah saw in my cousin Reese. She was a whiny brat who always tried to compete with me for everything, when I never played along. We were close in age and we used to be really close growing up, but she's always been jealous of the relationship I have with my parents and although I've never understood the hatred she has for me, I don't spend a moment harping on it. She was the one with the problem, not me.

"Here you are."

"Thanks. Now Camille—"

"Cam, please call me Cam. No one calls me Camille but my parents."

"Okay Cam, how have you liked being an attorney?"

"I love it, but it's all I've ever known, seeing that both of my parents are attorneys. For as long as I can remember, it's all I've ever wanted to do. What about you? What made you decide to become an attorney?"

"I guess you can say my desire to help people, because that's all I've ever known. My mom is a teacher and my dad is a police officer; both of them are very dedicated to their jobs."

"How did you meet Reese?"

"We were actually introduced through our best friends."

"How long have you been married?"

"Almost six months."

"That's great, I guess." I laugh.

"Why do you say that?"

"I just never thought she would get married. I mean, she's a brat."

"She's definitely that for sure, but I fell in love with her the moment I saw her."

"Awl, that's so cute."

He couldn't help but laugh.

"What's so funny?" Reese asks when she walks up.

"Nothing, I was telling Noah an old lawyer joke."

"Yeah okay," she says, rolling her eyes. "Where's your husband Cam? Don't tell me he has finally wised up and divorced you."

"Yeah, we've been divorced now for three years."

"Really?" Noah asks.

"No, but I thought I'd tell her that, so maybe she'll finally have an orgasm and loosen up."

"Fuck you Cam!"

"If only you weren't my cousin." I say, grabbing my drink to leave. "Because it'll probably do your snobby ass some good."

I get up to find my mom when I get a call from a restricted number.

"Hello."

"Is this Camille Shannon?"

"Who's asking?"

"This is Loren with the Channel 2 News. There has been talk that you may be chosen to fill Judge Sumner's seat in the upcoming election. You care to confirm or deny?"

"I have no comment."

"Is that because you may be going through a divorce?"

"What? Where did you hear that?"

"I can't reveal my source, but is it also true that your husband, attorney Thomas Shannon has a baby on the way?"

"What did you say your name was again?"

"Loren from the Channel 2 News and if you are willing to give me the scoop on your nomination details, we may be able to work out a deal."

"Well Loren from the Channel 2 News, call my office and leave your contact information with my assistant and we will talk when I get back."

What the hell was that?

After mingling with family and friends for way too long, I was over this party. "Mom, I think I'm going to call it a night. I'm really tired," I tell her when I finally find her and my aunt Sara.

"Are you sure honey? The party is just getting started."

"Yes," I said, giving her a kiss on the cheek. "I'll see you in the morning."

I stop by the bar for another glass of wine on the way to my room to take a hot shower. I couldn't get over how rude Reese was being. All through the night, she kept giving me the evil eye and the last thing I need after traveling all day, is a night of arguing with my bitch-ass cousin. I don't know what that chick's problem is, but if she continues to push me, I will definitely help her find a solution. I get to my room, undress and step in under the hot water in the shower. It really did my tense muscles justice. I didn't realize how tired I was until this very moment.

I step out of the shower and oil my body down in my body butter that I got from my favorite store back home, The Bubble Bistro. Slipping a gown over my head and grabbing my glass, I walk out of the bathroom to turn the cover down, just as there is a knock on the door.

"Mom, you in there?"

"Hey TJ, what's wrong?"

"Nothing. Grandma said you went to bed, so I wanted to check on you."

"That's sweet baby, but I am fine, just tired."

"You sure?"

"Yes, I'm sure. Go on back downstairs and enjoy the party."

"Okay. Goodnight. Love you," he says running back towards the stairs. He was gone before I had a chance to reply.

By the time I finally make it to the bed, I see a text notification on my phone from Thomas.

"Hey. I was checking on you and the kids to make sure you made it to your parents' house safely. Text me and let me know. I love you Camille."

Whatever! I said to myself while replying. "We are here. Thanks for checking on us, but we need to talk tomorrow. I got a call from a reporter, asking me if I was getting a divorce and if I wanted to confirm the news about your new baby."

"Reporter? Divorce? Baby? What the hell Camille?"

"The same thing I want to know, but we will talk tomorrow. I'm tired."

"Please call me tomorrow."

"I said I would."

"Thanks. I do love you Camille."

"Goodnight Thomas."

Just then another text comes through from Lyn.

"Can we please talk when you get back from Miami?"

"That depends on the topic Lyn."

"About us Cam."

"Us as friends?"

"Yes. I can get a room for us."

"We don't need a room to talk. We can do that over drinks in a restaurant."

"I was thinking more private."

"Goodnight Lyn."

"Please Cam."

Wow! I cannot believe Lyn is acting like this. I've got to call Ray.

"What's up chick, are you enjoying Miami?"

"We have a problem."

"What happened? Please don't tell me that bitch-ass Thomas is ruining your vacation?"

"No, it's Lyn. I think we need to stage an intervention or something."

"I know. I am worried about her too. I talked to Paul and he told me you called."

"Ray, I really think she is on drugs or something. I mean one minute she is talking crazy and the next, she is crying and asking for forgiveness. She needs help."

"I've been calling her, but she won't return any of my phone calls. I even went by the store, but she is never there."

"She needs help Ray. God! This is the last thing I need with everything I have going on!"

"Listen; enjoy your vacation with your family. We will figure this out here. I will call the other girls. If there is anything you need to know that can't wait until you get back, I will call you; otherwise, we will talk when you get back."

"Okay," I sigh, before hanging up the call and putting the phone back on the nightstand. I quickly say my prayers, because God is the only one who can get me through this mess.

# Chapter 24

"Good morning baby girl."

"Hey Daddy," I say, walking over to give him a kiss. "Where are Mom and the kids?"

"They went to work with her. She is finalizing all the details for that party thing she is doing tonight."

"Oh dang, the book signing. I need to go and find something to wear. I hadn't planned on going out."

"Yeah, because you know once your mom says something, there is no going back." He laughs.

"I know, right? What do you have planned for today?"

"I'm heading to play golf with a few of my fellow judges. Why, do you want to hang out? I can always cancel if you want to hang with big daddy."

"Big daddy huh? No big daddy, we have plenty of time to hang out. I guess I'll do a little shopping. Call me when you get done and maybe we can meet for lunch."

"Sounds good to me. Enjoy your day."

"Thanks big daddy. Love you."

"Love you too."

Walking out, I get another text from Lyn. "I'm sorry about last night. I would like to talk to you when you get back, and meeting at a restaurant is fine with me. Call me when you get back."

This motherfucker is losing it. I didn't even bother responding back.

***

I hate shopping. I don't know what it is about it, but it works my nerves. Usually I can go to Lyn's shop and let her style me, but she's not here and I am about to go crazy. I'm in the fourth shop after visiting three in the last forty-five minutes with nothing. Ugh!

"Are you okay?"

I look around stunned, because I hadn't realized I sighed so loud.

"Yeah, I'm sorry. I just don't like to shop," I said, turning to face the young lady. "Sam? Samantha King?"

"Camille Holden? Oh my God. What has it been, fifteen years since I've seen you?"

"Um, probably so. Wow, you look great." Damn she looks good enough to eat. Shit!

"So do you. How have you been?"

"I've been great. Is this your shop? It's very nice."

"Yes, thank you. I've been open here for about ten years now. Are you looking for anything in particular?"

"Yes, something for a party my mom is dragging me to tonight. My best friend has a shop back in Memphis and she is usually the one that styles me, because I don't like anything that has to do with shopping, unless I have to."

117

"I understand that. Well, follow me, because I have some exclusive pieces in the back that I'm sure will fit your body just right."

"Great."

"Now, tell me, what kind of party is it?"

"It's actually a book release or a book signing or something like that."

"Well, are you comfortable wearing shorts?"

"Yes, let me see what you have."

"I'll be right back. Can I get you something to drink? Some wine, coffee or water."

"Some wine would be great."

"Cool, I'll be right back."

"Cam, I laid a few outfits in the VIP dressing room straight back. Your wine is also there."

"Okay."

"Let me know when you have the first one on and I'll come in to see how it fits."

Walking into the dressing room, I was pleasantly surprised at the selections she had laid out. They were all my style. She was almost as good as Lyn. Taking a sip of my wine while I decided which one I would try first, I decided on this cute tangerine-colored sleeveless dress. It hugged my body in all the right places, but not too tight, so that it fit the occasion. The shoes were five-inch tangerine-colored stiletto sling backs with a black sole and white heel and they fit perfectly. By the time I was done, Sam was knocking on the door.

"Wow! I mean, shit girl, you are working this outfit," she said, laughing. "I have the perfect jacket. Be right back."

I was admiring myself in the mirror when she walked back in.

"Try this on," she said, handing me a white denim jacket that stopped right at my breasts. "Yes. Perfect."

"You get all the credit for this, because you picked my sizes perfectly."

"I have a trained eye for this, but your legs in this dress and those shoes. Whew!" she said, fanning herself.

"You think so?" I said, turning around.

"Yes ma'am. Do you want to try on the black shorts with the blue top?"

"No, I like this one right here, but I will take these other ones too. Who knows, I may find something else to get into while I'm here."

"How long are you staying?"

"Until Monday."

"Great. Maybe we can do lunch one day before you leave."

"That will be good."

"Okay, I'll get out of your way so you can change clothes. I will meet you up front."

# Chapter 25

"You can always stay. I don't mind you watching me undress," I say, as I pulled the jacket off.

"Um," she says clearing her throat. "I, um, I better not. My husband is on the way to take me to lunch."

"Are you sure?" I say, pulling the dress over my head, leaving only my black lace bra.

"You don't wear panties?" she asked, blushing.

"Not unless I have to and today was a day I didn't have to," I reply, looking at her as her eyes stop on my candy box that was as bare as a baby's bottom. I always make sure she is freshly shaven, because you never know when someone will need something sweet. I walk slowly towards her as she licks her lips. "Do you like what you see?"

"Hell yes, but I can't," she stutters as she backs up, until her back is against the door.

"What's stopping you? You can touch her if you want to. I won't tell. It'll be a secret worth keeping." I smile.

"I can't. I haven't been with a woman since—"

"Shh." Placing one finger over her lips while placing my foot on the couch that was inside the dressing room, I take her hand and slide it between my legs as I let my finger slide into her mouth. Moving to her neck, I use my tongue to trace up to her ear and I take it into my mouth.

Letting out a moan, I feel her relax as she inserts two fingers into me.

"How does she feel?" I whisper in her ear.

"Damn, you feel so good."

"Do you want to stop?"

"No, I want to feel you cum on my fingers."

"Are you sure? You might get hooked on this candy."

"Yes, I'm sure," she pants, pushing me back to the couch as she locks the door.

Lying back, I spread my legs wide for enough space to fit in and she goes straight for the goal.

"Ooo wee! Damn girl," I say, grabbing her head. "Oh, shit!" I moan as she sucks my clit into her mouth, sucking and slurping as if she's been missing the taste of pussy. I put both feet on the edge of the couch as I pull her head closer. She pulls away long enough to insert two fingers and she knows exactly where to place them.

"Cum for me, show me what you got," she commands.

"You may not be ready for that."

"Show me," she said as she pushed deeper.

"Oh!"

"Show me! Stop holding back."

I push her head up to look at her. "Are you sure? I thought you said your husband was on the way."

"He is and I am. Show me now!" s says between gritted teeth as her fingers turn and go deeper.

"Oh God, Oh God!" I scream out as quietly as I can as I squirt all over her hand and face.

"Um...I knew you had it in you." She smiles while licking up my juices.

"Sam, shit! Girl, I didn't know you had that in you though." I laugh. "You are a beast with the skills!"

"I have a few tricks up my sleeve." She smiles while standing up, wiping her mouth.

"I hope I don't have you late for lunch with your husband. What would he say if he knew you've already eaten?"

"You can ask him, because I'm sure he's watching."

"Really?"

"Yeah. From there," she says, pointing to a mirror.

"So that's why it's called the VIP room, huh? Okay, I ain't mad at you boo."

"I'll let you get dressed for real this time. There is a small bathroom behind that door. I will take these and get them ready for you to check out when you're ready."

After getting myself together, I grab my purse and head to the front of the store.

"You must be Cam?"

"That I am. And you must be Sam's husband."

"That I am. My name is Nick. Thank you for a great lunch time show," he said, smiling.

"You really should thank your wife, because she is one bad chick."

"I definitely know that, but I must say you taste damn good on my wife's lips."

"I know."

"Maybe we can hook up before you leave," he said as soon as my phone started ringing.

"I'll be sure to leave my number with Sam. It was nice meeting you, Nick. Hey Dad," I say, answering my phone.

"Hey, are you still shopping?"

"No, I am actually checking out now."

"Good. Your mom just called for us to meet for lunch at Garcia's downtown."

"Okay. I will be there in thirty minutes," I say before hanging up.

"You ready?"

"Yes I am," I say, handing her my debit card.

"Here is one of my cards. Call me before you leave, because from the look in Nick's eyes, he can't wait to taste you for himself."

"I sure will. Thank you again for everything."

"It was my pleasure to serve you."

# Chapter 26

We finally make it home from lunch and I was tired. I decide to take a shower and relax until I had to get dressed for this party my mom was dragging me to. As soon as I lay across the bed, my phone vibrates with a text from Thomas. I didn't even bother to read it.

"Mom," I wake up to Courtney standing over me.

"Hey, what's up?"

"Grandma sent me up to wake you up. She said the car will be here in two hours to pick y'all up for the party."

"Okay. Thanks."

"Oh and Dad called. He wants you to call him."

"Okay. Where is TJ?"

"He went with Aunt Sara."

"Oh Lord, there is no telling what she has him into. What are you going to do tonight?"

"Granddad is taking me to the movies."

"That sounds like fun."

"Not as much fun as you and Grandma."

"I'll switch with you." I laugh.

"You're up, finally."

"Yes Mom, I am up and I will be ready by the time the car gets here."

"Good. I don't want to be late."

"Okay, Okay."

"I'm out, don't forget to call Daddy," Courtney says, leaving my room.

I grab my phone to call Thomas, but decide against it. I didn't feel up to listening to him whine. I get up to lay out my clothes before I do my makeup. Thank God, I don't wear a lot and my hair is short and low maintenance.

Dang girl! I say to myself after looking at the finished look in the mirror. I put on some lip-gloss, grab my clutch bag and head for the door before my mom starts to yell my name.

"Wow Mom, you look great!" Courtney says when I come down the stairs. "Can I have that dress when you're done?"

"Thanks boo and of course you can. Where is your grandmother? I thought she would be at the door screaming my name by now."

"She is in her office on the phone."

"Tell her I will be in the den," I say as soon as my phone vibrates. I don't even have to look to know who it is.

"What's up Thomas?"

"Hey. I've been calling you all day."

"I know, what's up?"

"Nothing, I was just checking on you. Can't I do that without it being a problem?"

"Look, I am not in the mood to argue with you. I am about to go to a party with my mom and I don't need you ruining my mood. Can I call you back later, as in tomorrow?"

"Tomorrow? Dang, it's like that? I want to discuss that text you sent the other night."
"We will, tomorrow. Goodbye Thomas."

"Wow Camille, you look great," My mom says, coming into the den.
"Thanks Mom, so do you."
"The car is here. You ready?"
"Yes ma'am."
"Let's go."

# Party Time

"Wow Mom, this is great. You do this for all your clients?"

"Yes. If they work hard for themselves, I have no choice but to work hard for them and you will see that Johnie Jay is one hard worker."

"What book is this for him?"

"This is his fourth novel and it was a New York Times Best Seller before it even released."

"Wow, that's amazing."

"What does he write?"

"Erotica."

I almost choked. "Erotica? You represent an erotica author?"

"Yes, what's wrong with that? Sex sells Camille. Come and let me introduce you to him."

"Momma, please don't tell me he is an old white man with a big belly and beard."

"Oh child, he is far from that, but you'll see for yourself," she says with a smirk on her face.

"Sylvia," this fine specimen of a man says, before grabbing my mom up in a bear hug. Here I am, standing with my mouth open, because I'm trying to figure out if he's going to grab me next; good Lord this man is GORGEOUS. He has dreads that are hanging down past his shoulders; shoulders that are pumped up, biceps that I know can handle having these legs up and over them, tattoos that I wouldn't mind tasting and…

"This is my daughter, Camille Shannon. Camille, this is my bestselling author Johnie Jay."

"Camille," he says, letting my name roll off his tongue as he looks me over from head-to-toe, "it's nice to meet you."

"Johnie, please call me Cam and it's nice to meet you as well," I say, extending my hand while licking my lips, feeling sweat starting to form in all the right places.

"Cam, I see you inherited good looks from your mom, because you are as sexy as she is." He smiles.

"I did and I can see why this place is filled with women." I laugh.

"Why is that?" he asks as he slowly rubs his thumb over my hand.

"Because your ego is just as big as I hope your—"

"Okay, let's get this party started," my mom says, clearing her throat. "You two have all night to get acquainted."

"Cam, please don't leave until we have a chance to finish this conversation. I want to know what you hope is as big as my ego." He smiles.

"I wouldn't think of it. I'm going to find the bar," I say, walking off to leave them to whatever business they had.

After a few drinks and mingling throughout the party, I finally settle in a corner to watch my mom and I am in awe of her in her element. I know she is an awesome businesswoman, but it's been years since I've actually seen her in action and although we're at a party, it's no different. She's working the room like it's a courtroom and she has trained Johnie Jay well, because he is just as good. Yes, I've been watching him too. I had to laugh at myself just thinking about it.

I swing around on the bar stool and catch Johnie looking at me, so I decide to give him a show. I spread my legs slowly and run my hand under my dress. I didn't have to go far before it causes him to lose his train of thought, with the group of people he is speaking to. I turn around, fixing my dress and smiling.

"Something sure has you smiling."

"I'm sorry, I didn't hear you," I say to a random dude who interrupts my thoughts.

"I guess not, seeing that something has you deep in thought, care to share?"

"I was wondering if Johnie Jay actually tastes as good as he looks." I say.

"Well damn! Are you always this forthcoming?"

"Usually."

I guess I ruined his mood, because he grabs his beer and moves along.

Chapter 27

"Can I buy you another drink?"

"I am actually capable of buying my own. How about I buy you one?" I say to yet another dude who insists on bothering me.

"Hi, my name is Anthony."

"Cam."

"Cam, you are one gorgeous black woman."

"Thank you Anthony, but what brings you to a book signing?"

"My sister. She talked me into coming. She said I'd be able to meet some beautiful women and she was right. What about you?"

"My mother is the author's agent."

"Your mom is the agent of this dude?"

"Yes, why do you say it like that?"

"The way my sister talks about his books, all he writes about is sex."

"And what's wrong with that. Don't you like sex?"

"Yes, but I don't need a dude telling me how I need to please my girl."

"Is that what he's doing in his book, because I didn't think it was a how-to?"

"It's not but—"

"Then why are you threatened by a book unless you are threatened by the author?"

"I'm not threatened by him, I don't know him and I know how to please a woman," he says before standing, grabbing my face, and proceeding to tongue me down right there at the bar.

Smiling he says, "I have no issue pleasing a woman."

I grab a napkin and wipe my mouth before bursting into a laugh.

"What's funny?"

"The only thing that proved is that you can kiss like a teenager. Excuse me," I say, grabbing my purse.

"Mom, where is the restroom in this place?"

"There is an office in the back you can use," she says, pointing me the way.

Using the restroom, I was still laughing at whatever that was Anthony called himself doing at the bar. I washed my hands, fixed my hair and put on some more lip-gloss before opening the door to...

"Mr. Big Ego."

He pushes me back in the restroom. "Damn, you are one sexy woman Camille."

"Why thank you sir," I say, pulling him to me as I walk back into the restroom. I lean into the sink, raising my leg, allowing his hand to roam under my dress and he pulls down my thongs. He stops to smell them before placing them in his jacket pocket and before his hand begins to feel what he was doing to me.

"Damn girl, you are so wet. I want to feel the inside of you, now!"

"Hold on boo, you might get hooked on this good stuff. Are you sure this is what you want?"

"You need to be the one worried, because you're dealing with a freak," he says, inserting a finger into me. "Damn, this pussy feels good."

"I warned you." I moan as I push into his finger. "Mmmm."

"You like that baby?"

"Yes! Harder; more fingers, less talking."

"I'm in charge!" he says as his fingers goes deeper, causing me to lose my breath and my train of thought. He removes his fingers and replaces them with his tongue. "Oh my God!" I grab his head with one hand, and with the other one, I grab the sink. "Shit!"

"I'm cumming," I cry out as he pushes two fingers into me, intensifying my orgasm. "Damn boy!" He smiles when he thinks he's won. "That was pretty good."

"Pretty good? Is that all you got to say?" he asks as I stand up to fix my dress.

"Yeah."

"Meet me tonight," he says, washing his hands.

"I'll think about it." I say.

"I know you will," he says, handing me the envelope with his hotel key card in it that still had the room number on it.

"Uh, can I have my panties back please?"

"These belong to me now," he says, walking out.

***

"And where have you been?"

"To the restroom Mother," I say with a smirk on my face.

"For twenty minutes? And it just happened that Johnie disappeared at the same time."

"Really? I haven't seen him. Maybe he needed to use the restroom too. But I have to go. I left someone waiting at the bar."

"Whatever Camille!"

I left smiling. She knew I was lying. She could always tell when I was. I didn't know if

what's his name was still waiting or not, but I
had to go back to see, didn't want to be rude
and all.

"Anthony, you're still here?"

"Yes, I want to apologize for kissing you
earlier. I was out of line."

"It's cool. I know you were trying to
prove you're a manly man and all, but you
may want to work on your kissing skills before
you try that again."

"Damn, just kick a brother while he's
down."

"I'm not trying to be harsh; I'm simply
trying to stop you from embarrassing yourself
again. And you probably think you eat pussy
good too, huh?"

"I do, girl—"

"Boy stop! The way you kiss the lips up
top are the same way you kiss the ones below.
I don't know the type of women you've been
dealing with before, but either you make a lot
of money or they are naïve as hell."

I move closer to him. "Listen, a woman
wants you to take your time when you're
making her feel good. She doesn't want to feel
your teeth. She doesn't want to feel like she's
had a bath, and she doesn't want to hear you
slurping like it's all about you, because it
isn't. When you are kissing her lips, whichever
set you choose to kiss, it's all about her. Make
her remember you in her dreams when you're
done."

"Damn Cam, are you a sex therapist or
something?"

"No, I just know how I like to be pleased. Learn a woman's body, before you think you know how to please it."

"So you know a man's body well enough to please him?"

"Baby, I can have you cumming sitting right here at this bar with your clothes still on and my hands never have to touch you," I say as I lean closer to his ear, lowering my voice. "It's all about knowing what you want. I can take my tongue and start from your ear, make a trail down your neck, stopping to pay extra attention to your nipples, because you like for them to be sucked. Can't you feel the warmth of my breath on your chest? Then I move down to your belly button and linger there just for a moment, before I make my way down to the package I've been waiting to unwrap, feeling the softness of your pubic hair on my chin as I lick my lips in anticipation of—"

"Okay, stop!" he says, leaning away from me. I look down to see him hard as a rock. Not big, but hard.

"Come back to my place."

"I can't, I already have plans for tonight."

"Will you at least meet me for lunch before you leave town?" he says, handing me his business card.

"I'll think about it. It was nice meeting you, Anthony."

# Chapter 28

"Mom, I've had enough for tonight. I'm going to head out."

"Okay dear, do you want me to call the car for you?"

"No, I've called a cab. Don't wait up."

I stop by the bar to make a phone call before I walk out to the cab. "Hey, what's the address? Okay, I should be there in half an hour."

Yeah, I'd had enough of this type of party, but I was ready for another type that didn't involve books and definitely didn't involve my mom.

"Good evening, where to Ms. Lady?" the driver asks when he is back in the driver seat.

"Good evening to you. I'm going to this address," I say, showing him the napkin.

"No problem. This should be about a twenty minute drive."

"Cool."

We finally pull up to my destination, and the house is gorgeous. I pay the driver and before I make it to the front door Nick is already standing there looking good enough to eat.

"Cam, you are looking good this evening," he says, taking my hand as I enter the door.

"So are you. This is a beautiful home you have here."

"Thank you. Can I take your jacket and would you care for anything to drink?"

"Yes and yes. Where is Sam?" I ask, following him into the kitchen.

"She had to run over to one of the neighbor's house to fix her dress. She's having a big party tonight and something happened, so she called Sam hysterical. She'll be back any minute. You aren't uncomfortable here with me, are you?"

"Not unless I have a reason to be. Do you bite?"

"Not unless you want me to."

"I do, but only the right places."

"Where are those?

"Here," I say, pointing to my ear, "here," I say, pointing to my nipples, "and most definitely here," I say, pointing to my candy box.

"Is that right?" he asks as I notice his penis beginning to grow in his pants.

"Yes and obviously someone agrees with me," I say, as I walk over to him sitting on a bar stool at the kitchen counter.

"He has a mind of his own."

"Do you mind?" I ask.

"Not at all," he replies.

"I'm going to wait for your wife, but I just want to see what kind of equipment you're playing with, you can call it an inspection of sorts," I say, as I remove him from the basketball shorts he's wearing. "Not bad. May I?" I ask, as I kneel before him.

"Please do."

I carefully inspect him and his dick is chocolate brown, long with veins running through it. It's so thick and juicy, the right size to touch the back, side, top and bottom of every part of your insides! The kind that makes your mouth water just thinking about it. The kind that makes you licks your lips (like you're doing now). The kind that makes you come out of retirement just to give some head. The kind of dick that will make you leave work just to slob on it. Yes girl, that just how pretty this mane's dick is! I'm rubbing it up and down, because I want the feel of him all over my hands.

I lick my lips and I make sure my mouth is wet and slip him in, slowly! Yeah, I know I said I was going to wait for Sam, but I can't. He grabs the back of my head as I slide down on him, taking him all in.

"Um, you taste good." I say, standing up as he pulls me to him, kissing me. "If you keep this up, I won't be able to wait for your wife."

"Let me call her," he says, grabbing his cell phone. "Hey, Cam is here and we are trying to wait for you," he says while smiling at me. "Hell yeah, she looks good enough to eat. Here, she wants to talk to you," he says, handing me the phone.

"Hey girl." She tells me she wants me to start without her, because I'm Nick's anniversary gift and she's being purposely late. "No problem," I say, smiling. "I'll take good care of him until you get here."

I hang up the phone and lay it on the counter. "She says she'll be here in thirty minutes, but we can start without her. Can I shower first?"

"Sure. Follow me."

He leads me upstairs to their master bathroom and it is already laid out for a night of ecstasy.

"Everything you need should be in here and there's a robe hanging here for you."

"Great, I'll only be a few minutes."

After showering, I get out and oil myself up with some of Sam's edible body oil. I didn't even bother with the robe, because I wouldn't need it. I walk out the bathroom to Nick sitting on the side of the bed.

"Damn, Cam!" he says.

I walk over and stand in front of him, allowing him to roam over my body with his hands. He takes one of my nipples into his mouth as I caress his head. He then kisses down my stomach, before standing up for our mouths to meet.

"I need to feel you Cam."

"It's your party, baby. All you need is a condom."

He reaches over to the nightstand and quickly puts one on.

"How do you want it?"

"From the back."

I climb on the bed and get on my knees, before rubbing my candy box. I am anxious to see if he can use this pretty-ass cock like I'm hoping he can. Please be good!

He gets behind me and inserts a finger into me. "Hmm, you're so wet."

"Waiting for you."

He slowly rubs his cock against me before inserting part of himself in.

"Hmm," I moan.

"Am I hurting you?"

"No, don't stop," I say, as I push back for him to continue. He grabs my waist and again slowly slides in as I open my legs a little more. "Come on baby."

"I don't want to hurt you."

I move and turn around to face him. "Boy, if you don't stop playing and give me this dick. What's the problem?"

"Sam never lets me hit from the back, because she says I'm too big and it hurts."

"Do I look like Sam?"

"No."

"Exactly." I turn back around and position myself in front of him. This time he inserts himself into me and once he realizes he isn't hurting me, he grabs my waist and begins using that thang!

"Yes! Oh, that feels so good!" I say, spreading my legs a little more and lowering my back to give him full access to all of me.

He pulls to the end before pumping back in, gripping my waist tight and I'm gripping the sheets.

"Damn, this pussy is good," he says, before slapping my ass. "Lie flat," he commands and I obey.

This man is sending waves through my body and they feel amazing. "Don't stop!"

"I have no plans to," he says as he flips me over, spreading my legs as his tongue finds my clit.

"Oooh," I moan in sheer pleasure as his tongue is licking every part of me. He is sucking and slurping as if he is trying not to drop one drip of juice. He pushes open my lips and blows on my clit. "Shit boy!" I scream out, opening my eyes when I hear something, only to notice Sam sneaking into the room. She quickly notices me and motions for me to not say anything.

Shit, no problem! I can handle this dick on my own.

I grab his head and spread my legs to let him know I was enjoying what he was doing. He inserts his tongue into me as I make circles with my hips, making the sensation feel even better. "Um yes, make me cum."

He inserts a finger into me as he continues to suck on my clit. I slide my finger down to assist in getting me to my orgasm. I like how she feels when she is hot and wet. He takes my finger into his mouth as he slides another finger into me. "Cum for daddy. I know you want to," he says, playing my insides like they are his instrument.

My words are caught in my throat from the orgasm forming in my body; I don't even think I was breathing for a split second. "OH. MY. GOD!"

"Damn girl, you squirt too? Where have you been all my life? That shit is so sexy."

I pull him on top of me and insert him into me. "Less talking." I wrap my legs around him and grab his face to taste me on his lips. I take his tongue into my mouth as I moan my pleasure to what he is doing to my body, when I feel Sam slide into bed with us.

I look over at her and reach out my hand to bring her closer. Nick rises up, but never stops as Sam slides her tongue into my mouth. "Are you joining us now?"

"Just for the finale."

"That's enough, come closer and let me taste you." She climbs onto me, with her body facing Nick so that he can see her face, while I give her the pleasure she desires and I waste no time. As Nick is giving me what I need, I am giving it to Sam.

I take my time savoring her. I bury my face into her wet candy box and I suck and lick as if every second is giving her life.

"Oh shit Cam!" Sam screams out.

The more she screams the more Nick pounds into me and it feels so good. I moan into her pussy lips as I suck her clit, searching for the... "Oh God, right there! I'm cumming!" Sam screams before collapsing on the bed.

Nick presses my legs up to his shoulders as he groans through his orgasm before collapsing on top of me.

"Happy Anniversary you two." I smile.

I spend a few more hours with them before showering and heading home, promising to meet them for dinner before leaving town.

# Chapter 29

"What time did you get in this morning?" My mom asked when I finally came down.

"Hey to you too. Is there any coffee?"

"Yes, but you will have to make it yourself."

"Dang, you don't make a pot of coffee anymore?"

"No, that's what a Keurig is for. Now answer my question."

"I don't know Mom; I didn't think I had a curfew."

"You don't, but please don't tell me you were out with Johnie."

"Johnie? Why would you think that?"

"He left not soon after you did, so I assumed you two made plans to meet."

"Um, no! I was not with him last night."

"Good, I don't need to hear stories about you hitting it and quitting it."

"Mom!" I scream. "Where are Dad and the kids?"

"Who knows? When are y'all leaving?"

"Our plane leaves at ten Monday morning."

"Okay."

"Okay what?"

"Nothing."

"Mom, please don't tell me you've invited anyone over tonight. I just want a quiet dinner with you and Daddy on my last two nights here."

"Well too bad."

"You've already had a party."

"I know, but it's not often that I get to have you and the kids home, so I want to celebrate it. Is that too much to ask?"

"No Mom, party plan away."

I go outside on the patio to call Mr. Townsend.

"Hey Anita, is Mr. Townsend in?"

"Hey Camille, is everything okay?" he asks, after coming on the line.

"Yes sir, I was just calling to see if you've heard any news on the nomination?"

"Not officially, but I heard that the governor may announce his decision in two weeks."

"That soon?"

"Yes, he wants to get the seat filled. And listen; when you get back, I want you to meet my publicist, Carin Shields."

"Publicist?"

"Yes. She will be the one who will handle the media. It will be a fire storm once the governor announces your name as his recommendation."

"If, sir."

"When, Camille. Now, enjoy the rest of your vacation and I will see you on Tuesday. Have a safe trip back."

"Thank you Mr. Townsend."

"Did I just hear you on the phone with the old fart Townsend?" My dad asks, coming up behind me.

"Yes. And he says the governor may make his announcement in two weeks."

"Well don't sound so excited."

"I am excited, but I am also scared."

"That is understandable but enjoy the moment and deal with things as they come. I am so proud of you baby girl."

"Thank you Daddy."

"Have you told Thomas?"

"No, I'm about to call him now."

"Okay and Camille, stop worrying."

"Yes Daddy."

Okay, God. What have I gotten myself into?

I call Thomas and he answers the phone, sounding like he's fighting with it.

"Thomas?"

"Hello, hello."

"Thomas, what are you doing?"

"Hey, I was trying to answer the phone. How are you?"

"I'm good. How are you?"

"Better now that you've called."

"Listen, I called because I wanted to tell you that—" I start saying before I hear some girl call his name. "Who is that?"

He sighs. "That's Chelle."

"Is she at my house?"

"Yes, but she only came by to give me some information on her doctor's appointment."

"Are you kidding me? You got the nerve to have her in my house and then your dumb ass answers the phone. How stupid can you be?"

"Cam, it's not what you think."

"You need to be gone by the time the kids and I get back."

# Chapter 30

"Okay everybody, I want to make an announcement." My mom says, clicking her glass. "My baby girl has been nominated to fill a vacant position for circuit court judge in her district back home in Memphis."

"That's my girl!" My aunt yells out before running to give me a hug, almost knocking the drink out of my hand. "Speech, give us a speech."

"A speech Auntie really?"

"Yes girl, gone."

"Well, I know it's been a while since I've been home, but I have promised Mom and Dad that I will do better and I will. I have missed being with my family and friends and I have truly enjoyed being home these past few days. I don't know if I will get this upcoming position, but if I do, I know it isn't going to be easy, but I've learned from the best," I say, tipping my glass to my parents, "and I am looking forward to the challenge. But I hope if I win, all of you will come to Memphis to help me celebrate."

"You know I'll be there."

"Momma, why are you acting like she is someone important?" Reese asks, clearly jealous.

"She is."

"She ain't! Y'all are always pining over Cam. She ain't nothing or nobody."

"Girl, hush up." My Aunt Sara says.

"No, let her talk Auntie. She obviously has an issue with me and for years, I've been trying to figure out what it is. So tell me Reese, what is it? Why do you hate me so much? We used to be so close."

"Because you got everything. You got a daddy who loves you, the fancy house and clothes. All the boys wanted to be with Cam and you loved all the attention. For as long as I can remember, it's always about Cam and I am sick of it!"

"Girl, listen to yourself. We both grew up in this house. Whatever I had, you had. I never once made you feel less than me, because you weren't. I never asked for the attention from boys, I never wanted it nor desired it. You know that. You were the one that craved the attention and you can't be mad at me that you didn't get it, but that still doesn't explain the hatred you have for me now. You're a grown-ass woman."

"You screwed my boyfriend in college."

"What? Are you serious? What boyfriend?"

"Nathan."

"You've got to be kidding, right?"

"No! You knew I loved him and you slept with him and afterwards he never spoke to me again"

"Okay, that's enough you two." My mom says.

I start to laugh.

"It's not funny!" she screams.

"Yeah, it actually is. I don't know why we are even having this conversation now, when it should have happened years ago, but here you are, standing your skinny ass in the midst of a party, crying about something that happened over fifteen years ago. Girl, I never slept with that boy. He never spoke to your ass again, because he walked in on you screwing your roommate and her boyfriend."

"Oh my God!" Aunt Sara said. "So, you were a hoe. I never would have guessed it."

"She's lying."

"I have no reason to lie on you, but for you to treat me like trash all these years over this, is childish and stupid. You need to get a life. As a matter of fact, get your life! Come on Auntie, I need some tequila."

"I'm sorry baby. I don't know why that child of mine is acting so crazy."

"Auntie, you don't have to apologize for Reese. I am not thinking about her. I got so many other things to worry about than her and this mess."

"I know, but for that heifer to ruin your party."

"It's not ruined and after a few of these shots, I won't even remember her name."

I was right. After a few shots, Reese was the last thing on my mind as was Thomas and any other negative crap. I enjoyed the rest of the party before going to bed. I went to worship service on Sunday with my mom and dad and I really enjoyed it. They still attended the same church I grew up in. I went to dinner with Sam and Nick later that night; I promised them I would keep in touch and visit them whenever I came in town.

On Monday morning, I didn't want to say goodbye to my parents. I didn't realize how much I missed being at home until it was time to pack the car and head to the airport.

"You call me the minute you know something about the nomination," my dad says.

"I am sure, you will probably know before me."

"Call me anyway."

"And don't stay away this long again Camille," my mom says.

"I won't. You will be coming to Memphis to plan my celebration party, right?"

"Yes, but still."

"I know and I won't. I promise."

"Was it true what you said about Reese's boyfriend last night?"

"Yes Mom. I didn't sleep with that boy. He wasn't my type. He broke up with her because she cheated on him."

"I knew she was freaky."

"Mom!"

"What?"

"Nothing. I will call you before we board. I love you and Dad."

# Chapter 31

*"Home Sweet Home"*

As soon as we made it home, the kids ran straight to their rooms. I walk into the den to find Thomas kicked up on the couch.

"What are you doing here?"

"I stay here."

"You didn't understand what I said the other day on the phone when I said to find you somewhere else to go?"

"Camille, can we please talk?"

"Hold on," I say as soon as my phone began to vibrate. "Mr. Thompson, is everything alright?"

"Camille, I know we have a meeting scheduled for tomorrow, but I just received a phone call that I think you should know about."

"A phone call, sir?"

"Yes. I received a phone call from a young lady, who said she is pregnant by your husband and that he is divorcing you and marrying her. Is this true?"

I was so shocked by what he said that it took me by surprise.

"Camille, did you hear what I said?"

"Yes sir, I heard you. I'm just surprised that you would actually get a call about this. I cannot believe this."

"Why didn't you tell me?"

"To be honest sir, this is my personal business that I have no intention on allowing to interfere with my work, but I just found out before I left, so I really haven't had a chance to actually process it myself."

"Are you thinking about getting a divorce?"

"In all honesty, I don't know. Does this affect my chance on getting the seat?"

"Camille, let's slow down. We will cross that road when we get to it. Let the governor make his decision and if you decide to get a divorce, then we will let Carin deal with that. That's what I pay her for. Okay?"

"Okay and Mr. Thompson, I am so sorry about all of this."

"No need to apologize, shit happens. We will talk more tomorrow. Get some rest."

I hang up the phone to Thomas looking at me crazy. I had tears streaming down my face and I didn't know what to do or say to him.

"Camille, what happened?"

"Ask your baby momma. Apparently she called my boss to tell him about the plan for y'all to be a happy family."

"What? She did what?"

"Did I stutter?" I ask, standing up.

"Baby, please wait."

"Thomas, don't touch me. I need to leave before I say or do something that I will regret."

"Where are you going?"

"Minding my fucking business!"

\*\*\*

It was still early, so I end up calling Dr. Scott instead. I don't know why, but she was the first person I thought of.

"Cam, I was surprised to get your call. Is everything okay?"

"I don't know why I called you or even why I am here. I will come back tomorrow for our regular scheduled appointment," I say, grabbing my purse to leave.

"Camille, stop running. Please sit down and tell me what's wrong."

"Can you believe that Chelle, Thomas's crazy-ass baby momma called my boss and told him that she was pregnant by Thomas and he was leaving me and marrying her?"

"And how does that make you feel?"

"Again with that dumb ass question? It makes me feel like singing "Happy" by Pharrell. What do you think? It pisses me off."

"Finally. An honest answer."

"Well, I guess therapy finally worked."

"Camille, Cam; be for real for a moment. We are long from done. Now that you are pissed, what now?"

"I don't know. I was on the verge of asking for a divorce, but now that I am nominated for a vacant judge seat in my district, I just don't know. I do know that I cannot continue to allow the mess that Thomas made to affect everything I've worked so hard to build."

"But Thomas didn't make this mess by himself."

"Who else did?" I ask, looking at her.

"You did."

"Me?" I laugh. "You want me to take the blame for him getting her pregnant? Okay, you're just as crazy as she is."

"I'm not saying you are to blame for her being pregnant, but you brought her into your lives, so aren't you to blame for that?"

"I've already taken the blame for that. Shit! How many times are we going to beat that dead topic? We both know I brought her in, but I didn't make him sleep with her without protection. I damn sure won't take the blame for the shit he has gotten himself in and the hell she is causing now, so if you think I should, then you can ride the same boat to hell with them," I tell her, grabbing my purse as I head for the door.

"Cam, please wait. Don't leave like this. Stop running away. Let's finish the session."

At this point, I didn't give a damn about the session or her.

# Chapter 32

As soon as I walk out of Dr. Scott's office, I get a call from a blocked number.

"Hello."

"How can a hoe become a judge?"

"Who is this?"

"How can a hoe become a judge?"

"Stop playing on my phone, I am not in the mood!"

I hang up as I walk to the car, only to get there to find an envelope on my windshield. What the hell is this? I open it to find my medical records from when I was in the hospital a few years back, showing that I had cocaine in my system, pictures of me in a bikini, a few of me half-naked that I had never seen before and a note that said, "IS THIS A FUTURE JUDGE?" Really?

I get in the car and throw them all on the seat. I call Charles and tell him about the package. He says he will meet me at the office tomorrow morning to take care of it. I hang up and my phone vibrates with a blocked number again.

"Stop calling me."

"Cam, it's me, Lyn."

"Lyn, did you call me a few minutes ago from a blocked number?"

"No, this is my first time calling you. What's wrong?"

"Nothing, what's up?"

"I was calling to see if you wanted to meet me for drinks. I was leaving the shop and I knew you were back from vacation and—"

"How did you know we were back?'

"I...uh...Kelsey told me."

"Look Lyn, not tonight. I will call you later on."

"Why do you keep blowing me off?"

"What?"

"You heard me? You find time for everybody else but me. You found time for Dr. Scott, why can't you find—"

"Are you following me?"

"I am just asking you to have a drink with me."

"Goodbye Lyn."

I make it home in a state of confusion. I don't understand what is going on. It seems like everything is happening all at once. Okay Lord, what's next?

I walk in the den to find Thomas pacing and drinking.

"Camille, are you okay? Where have you been?"

"Why are you concerned?"

"Cam, wait before you leave; can we please talk?" he asks, trying to grab my arm.

"Thomas, don't touch me. What is there to talk about?"

"Can you please for one second just listen?" he screams. "I don't believe Chelle would do this."

"Hold on partner! Lower your voice, because I don't have to do shit. Do you honestly think I am about to stand here and listen to you defend your baby momma?"

"I am not trying to defend her, but I haven't had any contact with her and I don't believe she would do it."

"Oh okay. Cool, I'll take your word for it and I'll sit back and allow this hoe to ruin my life. I worked too hard to watch it be blown away by a jealous baby momma, who wants the baby daddy to herself. She can have you boo."

"Just let me call her."

"I don't give a damn who you call."

"Just let me talk to her, please," he says, grabbing his phone and putting it on speaker.

"What's up baby daddy? I thought you didn't want to talk to me?" Chelle says, answering the phone."

"Chelle, did you call Cam's boss?"

"What?"

"Did you call Cam's job and tell her boss that you were pregnant with my baby, and that I was leaving her and marrying you?'

Laughing, she says, "Hell no. Why would I jeopardize her job, when we have a baby on the way that she has to help take care of? Man, I ain't crazy. I know she pays for y'all to live like that."

"Are you sure you didn't call her job?"

"Didn't I just say I didn't? I ain't got to lie. Look baby daddy, I know you got a job, but your wife pays to be the boss and we both know that she will be the one taking care of me and this baby, so I ain't about to mess that up."

"Did you bust the window out of her car?"

"Hell no, who the hell do you think I am? This ain't no Lifetime movie. It's bad enough I was blamed for filing that damn police report, I'm still dealing with that shit!"

"Please don't take offense if I don't believe you," I say.

"Well, I am not sure what else to tell you. I am not about to jeopardize your job, when you have to take care of this baby."

"You are crazy as hell if you think I am taking care of anybody other than the two I pushed out. The one you're having is between you and Thomas."

"We will see." She laughs.

"Yes we will."

"Okay, Chelle. I will talk to you later."

"Wait. Are you going to the doctor with me for the four-month checkup or not? I may be having an ultrasound."

"I'll let you know," he says, before hanging up.

"Camille, I don't know what is going on here, but let me help you figure this out."

"If I need your help, I'll let you know."

I get up and go to our bedroom. I get undressed, get in the shower, and for the first time in a long time, I cry. I don't know why, but it is what I need. Afterwards, I get out, oil myself all over and slip on a nightgown; say my prayers and get in the bed. Tomorrow has to be better.

# Chapter 33

"How was your trip boss lady?"

"It was great. It felt so good being home. I didn't realize how much I missed my mom and dad, until I actually saw them."

"I know. Being that far away from them has to be hard. I have your schedule for the day and your coffee."

"Great. Is Mr. Thompson in yet?"

"No, he won't be in today, but he called and said if you need to reach him to call him at home."

"Okay. Thanks Stephanie. Anything else happen while I was away?"

"Nothing I am sure you haven't been made aware of." She laughs. "Oh, Judge Alton was added to your calendar at four this afternoon."

"Great. Okay, close the door for me."

Checking my email, I see the invitation from Monica, inviting me to her book release party. Hmm... It makes my mind wonder back to Miami and that fine-ass Nick and his sexy wife Sam. I pick up the phone to call Ray.

"Raylin, what's up boothang?"

"Bitch, where have you been? I am kicking your ass when I see you. I thought I was going to have to put out an APB for your black ass."

Laughing, I say, "I missed you too."

"Whatever! What's up chick, how was Miami?"

"It was great and baby we've got to go back soon, but look, I'm calling to see if you and the girls want to go with me to a party Saturday."

"A party or a 'party' party?"

"No, just a party. This new client named Monica Walker is having a book release party and she invited me and said I can invite my girls, but you will never guess who she is married to."

"Who?"

"The District Attorney, Brent Walker."

"Brent Walker. Why does that name sound familiar?" Ray asks.

"He was one of the guys from the party we all went to a few years ago, remember? He was the one Chloe turned out."

"For real? Oh shit, this is going to be fun."

"I know I hope she comes. You know she is such a good girl now, she might not come if you tell her he's going to be there."

"Who said I was?"

"You sneaky heifer. Well, don't tell her. It'll be funny to see if he recognizes her."

"Cool."

"By the way, did you and Shelby talk to Lyn? Do you know she called me the other night asking why I keep blowing her off? I think she was following me."

"Are you serious? That motherfucker is crazy Cam; please stay away from her. We haven't had a chance to talk to her because she won't return any of our phone calls.

Something is definitely going on with her though. I thought about calling Paul. I didn't want to get involved in their house business but I think I will today. Are you inviting her to the party?"

"Hell no! She is going through something and she needs some help, Ray. I talked to Paul before I left and told him I would get with you all about a possible intervention or something."

"I am down for that, because that sister has gone off the deep end for real, but it'll all work out. In the meantime, send me a text with the details for the party."

"K. I'll talk to you later."

I hang up from Ray and go over the rest of the emails I have and a few reports on my desk. I call Monica and accept her invite, before replying to a text from Jyema who I was meeting later tonight. I was just about to head to lunch, when I get an instant message from Raul, saying he was heading to my office.

"Hey boss lady."

"Hey Raul, what's up?"

"I have some information on your friend Lyn. I ran a background and financial check on her, which checked out. I followed her on a few occasions and a few times she—" he trailed off.

She what?

"She was following you."

"Following me? Why didn't you call me Raul?"

"I was taking it as her being your friend and maybe you all were going to the same place, but then she would just sit and watch you. She is crazy."

"I am agreeing with you. What about while I was out of town?"

"She was quiet and to herself. She was with another lady, a pregnant lady a few times. They met at a coffee shop not far from your house."

"A pregnant lady? Do you know who she is?"

"No, but I have some pictures. I will have them sent over to you in a few days, but this lady needs to be watched. I will send you my final report with the pictures. Do you want me to stay on her?"

"No. That's enough for now. I am going to meet with her husband and my other friends about an intervention soon, so if I need you, I will let you know. Send me your bill and I will take care of it."

"Okay and I will get the report and pictures sent over."

I sat back in my chair replaying Raul's words, when Stephanie buzzed to let me know Mr. Thompson was on the phone.

"Mr. Thompson, how are you?"

"Camille, I have great news."

"Okay," I say, kind of hesitantly.

"The Commercial Appeal is running the story tomorrow about the nominations listing the names of the three finalists that were submitted to the governor."

"Really?"

"Yes, and I heard that Governor Haslam is going to make his announcement soon, because he wants the seat filled immediately."

"Great. So we should know something soon, huh?"

"Yes, I would say in about two weeks."

"Wow."

"Yes, I know. How are things at the office?"

"Everything is going great. How is your day off? You don't take those often."

"It is going great. The old wife made me take off. How are things at home?"

"They are okay but don't worry, they won't affect my work ethics."

"I am not worried about that; I am concerned about you, but let's schedule to get together soon with Carin, my publicist."

"Okay, sounds good. Now, enjoy your day off."

# Chapter 33

"Hey."

"Hey yourself, you are looking good tonight," Jyema tells me when I walk into the hotel room. "What's wrong?"

"Nothing, I just have a lot on my mind."

"Come on over and let me take your mind off of whatever else you're thinking about," she says, taking my hand and leading me to the bed.

She pushes me back on the bed and begins kissing me. Damn she tastes good. She moves to my neck and then over to my ear. That's my spot. She moves her hand under my skirt and...

"Stop."

"What?"

"I'm sorry, but I am just not in the mood tonight."

"Just lie back and let me get you there baby. I promise I can get you in the mood."

"Not tonight."

"Come on Cam. It's been weeks since I've tasted you. Please baby."

"I know and I'm sorry, but I can't. I will make it up to you."

\*\*\*

"Mom! Mom!"

"TJ, why are you screaming?" I ask, as we all run into the kitchen.

"You are on the news! Look!"

"The Shelby County Judicial Commission has submitted the names of three attorneys to Governor Bill Haslam to fill the vacancy created by Circuit Court Judge Sumner who had to retire, due to illness. The commission has nominated attorney Aubrey Holman, attorney Patrick Kenlee and attorney Camille Shannon to fill the seat on the bench. Governor Haslam has sixty days to select one of the three finalists and the selected individual will fill the seat until the next general election."

"Oh my God, Mom! You looked great in that picture too. I can't wait to tweet this!" Courtney squeals!

"See, I told you," TJ says, lowering the volume on the television.

"Yes you did. Now finish getting ready for school before you're late," I tell him as my cell phone begins ringing.

"Bitch, you are a superstar now!"

"Hey Raylin." I laugh.

"I am so proud of you."

"Thanks girl. Now, the real madness begins."

"You were made for this. I will talk to you later; I just wanted to congratulate you."

After texts from the other girls and a few block calls that I ignored, I am finally able to get dressed when Thomas walks in the room.

"Camille, I am very proud of you."

"Thank you, Thomas."

"Look at me for a moment."

I turn to look at him standing in the door.

"I really am proud of you. I know that we are having our issues, but please don't allow them to diminish who you are in your field of work. You make me proud to be your husband when you set foot in any courtroom and today, I will say it again; I am proud of you Camille Shannon."

He walks over and kisses me and for a moment, I forget about everything and I remember why I fell in love with this man. The tears that are streaming down my face are liquid prayers from my heart to God's ears that He works this thing out in our favor starting from today. When Thomas releases me, he turns and walks away and I just stand there a minute to get myself together.

I finally leave the house and make it to the office.

"Congratulations boss lady," Stephanie says when I walk in.

"Thanks. How has it been around here?"

"Crazy. You've had a lot of people stop by. Judge Alton called and Mr. Thompson is waiting for you in his office."

"Already?"

"Yes. Do you want your coffee now?" She laughs.

"Yes, please!" I answer as I place my purse and computer bag on the desk.

She hands me my coffee as I make my way to Mr. Thompson's office. Anita is at her desk and she beckons for me to go on in.

"Camille, did you see the news this morning?" Mr. Thompson asks, with a huge smile on his face.

"Yes sir, I did."

"Are you excited?"

"I am very excited. How long do you think it will be before Governor Haslam makes his announcement?"

"I have it on good authority that he will make it within the next two to three weeks, which is why I want you to meet, Carin Shields."

"Good morning, Camille. I've heard so many good things about you."

"Good morning, but please call me Cam."

"Cam, I am a publicist and I am here to write a press kit on you, something that we can release to all the major media outlets once the governor makes his announcement known. It'll be a few pictures of you, of you and your family, and almost a resume of sorts. Something to let the public know who Camille Shannon really is."

"Okay but listen, I did get a call from a lady at Channel 2 News while I was in Miami. She was asking questions about me being nominated and about some personal business that she shouldn't have known."

"What was her name?"

"I can't remember, but I can ask Stephanie, because I told her to call and leave her information here at my office."

"What type of personal information did she have?"

"My husband has been having an affair and may have a baby on the way. She knew this, which means someone has been feeding her information."

"I will find out. You let me worry about that. Do you have a recent professional headshot?"

"Yes, we had some done a few months ago for the firm."

"Great. Send me a copy. If you have a recent one of you and your family, send me that too."

"Wow, that's it?"

"Yes, I told you. Let me take care of any negative issues. Is there anything else I need to know about?"

"No." Then I remembered, "Wait, there is something else. I haven't even told Mr. Thompson about it yet, because it slipped my mind with everything going on. Someone left an envelope with some pictures of me, my medical records from a couple of years ago when I was in the hospital, and a note on my car a few weeks back; oh, and my window was broken out a few nights ago."

"Where is the envelope?"

"In my office."

"Does anyone else know about this?"

"Judge Alton. I told him about the envelope, but he and I never got a chance to meet about it, and Stephanie."

"I will stop by and get it on my way out. Was anything taken when your window was broken?"

"No, they just left another note."

"Do you still have it?"

167

"I think so. I will look when I get back to my office."

Is there anything else I need to know about?"

"Not unless there is anything you want to know about."

"I think this is all I need for now. If there is anything else I need, I will call you. If you think of anything, take my card and call me at any time."

"Great. Thank you Ms. Shields. Mr. Thompson, is there anything else you need from me?"

"No, but please don't hesitate to let me or Carin know if you need us. I don't care what it is."

"Thank you both."

I make it back to my office and get all of the information together for Carin. I finally get a chance to sit down at my computer to check my email, when I see one from Sam, which makes me think of her fine-ass husband. Whew, Lord. It is just a normal check-in email, but I quickly send her one back, letting her know I need her to find me something cute to wear for my celebration party when I am selected for this position. I'm claiming it.

I hear a knock on the door and look up to see Carin. I close my laptop and stand up to meet her.

"Hey, I left everything with Stephanie."

"I know, but I wanted to stop in and make sure you are really okay with everything."

"Come in," I say, motioning for her to have a seat.

"I've worked with Mr. Thompson for over ten years, so I know when he believes in someone and Cam, he truly believes in you."

"I know and I truly appreciate everything he has done for me, and I don't want to let him down, but someone is trying really hard to sabotage my chance at this."

"Do you have any idea who it is?"

"Honestly, I thought it was the chick that my husband was having the affair with, but she swears it's not her, and then my best friend has been acting crazy, so I had Raul investigate her, but I don't know."

"Well, I'm going to look into it, but in the meantime, you need to focus on doing what you do best, which is your job. You let me handle the rest."

"I am trying Ms. Shields but—"

"Call me Carin."

"I am trying Carin, but the last thing I want is to be crucified in the media."

"I understand that, but that's why Mr. Thompson pays me well. I know it's easier said than done, but you need to let me worry about this."

"I will try. Thank you again, Carin."

"Again, if you need me; don't hesitate to call. You can reach me at any time, day or night."

# Chapter 34

*Party with the ladies*

"Divas! Are you ready to party?" I ask, walking into Shelby's house.

"Hell yes!" Ray says.

She is standing there with these white skintight cut up jeans that had her ass banging, a white tee and a white jean jacket with these studs on the shoulders. Her shoes were some colored stiletto heels that set the entire outfit off.

"Damn Ray, you rocking that outfit boo! Shit!"

"Thank you girl. Anthony was looking upside my head when I left the house tonight." She laughed. "You aren't looking bad yourself."

I had on some black leather joggers, a white sheer shirt with a red tank underneath and red, black and white stilettos.

Shelby wasn't short, stopping with her black leather leggings, embellished tee and baby blue blazer and matching heels. Even pregnancy couldn't stop her from looking fierce.

Kerri was still on maternity duty, so she was sitting this one out and Lyn's ass was not invited. "Where is Chloe?"

"Here I am," she says, coming down the hall in a black dress that is cut down the front and hugging every curve in her body, with some red five-inch stiletto pumps that made you notice the muscles in her calves.

"Well damn."

"What?" she ask, stopping in her track.

"Where in the hell has this chick been?" I ask, looking at her up and down.

"Shit, I am excited about getting out of the house. Let's go!"

The party is being held at the Memories Banquet Hall. We park and head inside. It felt good to be heading out with the girls. Even if it's not all of us, it still feels good. When we make it inside, the party is in full swing and it is very nice. I notice Monica, so I walk towards her when she looks up.

"Cam, I am so glad you could make it. You look great."

"Thank you. Let me introduce you to my girls. These are my best friends, Shelby, Raylin and Chloe."

"Hello ladies, it is so nice to meet you. Thank you all for coming tonight, let me introduce you to my husband." She turns to grab him. "Babe, I want you to meet the new attorney I was telling you about. This is Camille Shannon and her friends."

When he turned around, it was as if he had seen a ghost.

"Cam, this is my husband, Brent Walker."

"Brent, it is so nice to meet you. These are my best friends; Ray, Shelby and Chloe."

171

Chloe was the first one to speak with a smile, "It's nice to meet you, Brent."

"Uh, it's nice to meet you ladies. Can I get you anything to drink?"

"Yes," Ray says. "Some wine would be great."

"I'll walk with you," I tell him.

By the time we make it to the bar, I can tell he is dying to say something.

"Cam, how long have you known my wife?"

"I met her when she hired my firm for some legal work."

"Mane, this is crazy. Chloe still looks great," he says, looking over at her. "Did you know Monica was my wife?"

"I had no idea until she invited me to this party. Why? Is there a problem?"

"I mean, we did sleep together, well not you and me, but you know what I mean."

"I don't know what you're talking about and I suggest you forget what you're talking about as well," I say, grabbing three glasses and walking off.

I make it back to the girls and Monica has a table set aside for us; she is still there talking to Ray and Chloe, when I interrupt with wine.

"Here are the drinks. Monica, this place looks great. Where can I purchase your book?"

"I have a table set up over there in the corner, but you don't have to buy one. I have gift bags for you and your friends."

"Thanks, but please allow us to still purchase one to at least give away or something, because we love to support each other's gifts."

"Okay. We can take care of that later. In the meantime, you all enjoy the party. I'm going to mingle for a minute, but I will be back in a bit."

"She seems like a cool chick," Ray says.

"I only know her business wise. This is the first time I've seen her outside of the office, but yeah, she seems cool. I like her. What about you, Chloe?"

When she didn't answer, I see it's because she is too busy making eyes with Brent.

"Uh, Chloe?"

"Huh?" she asks, smiling.

"Huh, hell," Ray says. "I know Ms. 'I's married now', isn't making eyes at somebody else is she?"

"I am not. I was just admiring the many people here at the party."

"That bullshit and you know it. Girl, quit tripping. You need some new dick, admit it," I say, looking directly at her. "I'm not going to judge you."

"Fine, you're right. Please don't cuss me out Cam."

"Why would I cuss you out?"

"The way I treated you, I deserve it."

"Girl, we all mistakes. I'm just glad you finally see that my mistakes are no bigger than yours."

"I know and I'm sorry Cam. I get it now. I love Todd, but with everything he has going on, the sex is lacking and I've tried to talk to

173

him about it. I've bought toys, I masturbate two times a day, but that shit ain't getting it."

"Girl, we feel you!" Ray says, laughing.

We were about to finish the conversation, but the Wobble begins to play and that was our cue to hit the dance floor.

After dancing through three line dances, Ray and I make our way over to the bar before going back to the table. Somewhere in between dance two and three, we lost Chloe. We thought she may have gone to the bathroom, but now I am thinking her sneaky ass is up to no good.

"Have you ladies seen my husband?" Monica asks, walking up.

"No, but we just came from the dance floor." I answer.

"Okay, I've been looking for him to get a picture. Anyway, Cam; let me get a picture with you and your girls."

"Chloe just went to the bathroom." Ray lied. "Why don't we go and buy those books and she should be back by the time we are finished."

"Sounds like a plan," she says, still looking around for her husband.

I pull out my phone to text Chloe.

"Where in the hell are you?"

No response.

We make it over to the area to buy a few of Monica's books.

"So Monica, what is the new book about?" Ray asks, to buy some time while I text Chloe's ass again.

"Bitch, I know you got my text."

"OMW!"

OMW, really? I am sure Ray wasn't paying attention to anything Monica was saying, but she had to take one for the team. Chloe finally walks up, smiling and shit.

"I hope it was worth it," I whisper to her.

"Oh, it was." She laughs.

"Okay ladies, now if I can get a picture with all of you for my website," Monica says after we all pay her for our book, as her husband walks up with a beer in his hand.

"Babe, where have you been?" Monica asks him.

"I got hemmed up by an old friend. I'm sorry."

"Monica, we're going to go. Thank you for the invitation. We really enjoyed ourselves."

"Yes, this was a great party," Chloe says.

"Thank you. I am so glad you enjoyed it. Thank you for coming."

"You are welcome. I'm glad I came too," she replies, looking at Brent who chokes on his beer.

# Chapter 35

"How are you tonight Camille, I mean Cam?"

"I am great Dr. Scott. How are you?"

"I am well. I haven't seen you since the last time you stormed out of here, how have things been?"

"The same as always. My husband still has a baby momma, I still have someone trying to ruin my career, a crazy-ass friend who claims to be in love with me, a nomination for a job of a lifetime hanging over my head and I am still dealing with this therapy shit. So, things have been great," I say sarcastically.

"And what are you doing to change anything that you don't like?"

"Well, let's see. I can't kill the husband and baby momma, because I'll end up in jail and on an episode of "Snapped". I don't know who my stalker is, I've distanced myself from the best friend, I am waiting on the announcement for the job and I am almost done with therapy."

"Are you still cheating on your husband?"

"Define cheating?"

"Are you still sleeping with other people outside of your marriage?"

"See, I don't consider that cheating."

"Does your husband know about it?"

"I'm sure he does."

"And because you are sure he knows you don't qualify it as cheating?"

"It doesn't qualify as cheating, because I say it doesn't."

"That makes no sense. You want to make rules up as they go to fit Cam and it doesn't work like that. You are an attorney; you know the difference between right and wrong. Are you a Christian?"

"Yes. What does that have to do with anything?"

"Do you not take your vow to God serious?"

"Of course I do, that's why I repent for the mistakes I make. I am not perfect, I never said I was."

"But does repentance give you the right to do the same sin over and over?"

"I thought this was therapy and not Sunday school. I don't need you to lecture me on what the Bible says. I know what it says. I know what I do is wrong, but God says He will forgive me every time I fall, if I get up and ask for forgiveness."

"Yeah, but at some point Cam, aren't you tired of falling? When is enough going to be enough?"

"When I've had enough. Is our time up?"

"Yes. Will I see you on next week?"

"Maybe or maybe I've had enough."

# Chapter 36

## One Month Later - Life Changing Call

It's been a month and everything seems to have smoothed out. Governor Haslam still hasn't announced his pick for the vacant seat yet, but we are expecting it any day now. I haven't had any new issues with my "stalker" other than the occasional blocked calls. I guess they are waiting on the announcement too. Yes, I am still holding on and still going to therapy. Dr. Scott gets on my nerves, but she's right about a lot of things. Thomas and I are, well, we are just us. He still has his baby momma drama. I ain't bout that life. My mom and dad are coming here in two weeks for spring break and I am so excited.

Oh, Lyn has been missing in action lately. I don't know what is up with her. She is still running her store and talking to Kelsey, but she won't have anything to do with Paul or us. She sends me a text, but if I refuse to meet her, she flies off the handle and then its weeks before I hear from her again. We tried to do the intervention thing, but she never showed. She is grown and you can't help someone who doesn't want to be helped. I have too many other things going on; other than to chase after someone, trying to force help down their throat.

"Stephanie, can you pull the case file for Blake vs. Crawley for me?"

"Sure thing, I will bring it right in."

I get a text from Jyema, confirming our meet-up for tonight. I quickly reply when Stephanie comes running in with the file and a look of excitement on her face.

"What's wrong?"

"Governor Haslam's office is on the line."

"Really?"

"Yes, pick it up!"

"This is Camille Shannon."

"Please hold for Governor Haslam."

"Mrs. Shannon."

"Yes sir, Governor Haslam."

"How are you today?"

"I am great, sir. How are you?"

"I am great. I won't hold you long, but I wanted to call and officially offer you the seat of Circuit Court Judge District Seven. I am very impressed by your qualifications young lady and I know you will serve the seat well."

"I will indeed sir."

"The official announcement will be released within the hour and afterwards my office will call with the official swearing-in and other details later. Congratulations Mrs. Shannon."

"Thank you, sir. Thank you for an amazing opportunity."

"You've earned it."

"Oh my God, Stephanie!" I scream as she begins jumping up and down. "Can you please get my husband on the line?"

Mr. Thompson and Carin walk into my office with champagne. "I should have known you would already know."

"The press kits have already started going out. Congratulations, Cam," Carin says.

"I am so proud of you Camille," Mr. Thompson says, coming over to give me a hug.

"I couldn't have done this without you."

"Cam, your husband is on line one."

I step over to my desk. "Hey, I wanted to call you first with some amazing news. I got the seat."

"Oh my God baby, that is great! I am so proud of you. Are you staying at the office, I can come there."

"Yes, please do. I will wait for you."

"I am on my way."

I grab my phone and call my dad. "Daddy," I say, with tears streaming down my face.

"I already know baby girl and your mother and I are so very proud of you. Go on and enjoy the moment. Call us when you make it home."

I hang up, because between the tears and the noise that was now in my office, I couldn't say a word. I send out a quick text to the girls and then make my way back over to Carin and Mr. Thompson.

"How does it feel?"

"It hasn't sunk in yet."

"Well get ready."

"Yes ma'am. The swearing-in will most likely take place in two weeks. You'll be sent all the details, so that you can invite your family and friends," Carin says, as I feel someone come up behind me.

"Thomas."

"Baby, I am so proud of you," He says, sweeping me up into a hug.

"Thank you," I say, hugging him extra tight. When he finally puts me down, I say, "You remember Mr. Thompson and this is Carin, my publicist."

"Mr. Thompson, it is nice to see you again sir and Carin, it's nice to meet you. I am sure you're preparing for all of the news trucks that I saw pulling up outside."

"News trucks?" Stephanie says.

"Already?"

"Yes, the real fun begins now," she says, "but you let me handle that."

Judge Alton walks in with a few of the other partners and associates offering their congratulations.

"Judge Alton, thank you for coming," I say, as he gives me a hug.

"I wouldn't have missed it. Congratulations, Mrs. Shannon. A well-deserved honor."

"Absolutely. Everyone grab a glass," Mr. Thompson says. "To Camille, we here at Thompson and Associates could not be more proud of you for all that you've accomplished. I have no doubt that you will make one hell of a judge, because you never slack at being an attorney. We raise our glass to you today and please know that we love you here and will always have your back. To Judge Camille."

"Judge Camille!"

Thomas turns and kisses me and I can feel Charles's eyes burning a hole in my back.

We stay in the office celebrating with my associates for the next hour.

"Let's get out of here so that we can really celebrate," Thomas whispers in my ear.

"But babe, everybody is still here." I laugh.

"Go ahead you two; I know you probably want to celebrate with your family," Mr. Thompson says.

"Thank you. I will see you in the morning," I tell him.

"Or Wednesday. You can take the day off if you want."

"Of course not," I say.

When I make it to Thomas's car he is almost skipping. "Where are we going?"

"It's a surprise."

He opens the door and I get in. It is only about seven in the evening, so I have no idea what he has planned, or what he could have planned so quickly. We didn't drive, far before we make it to the boat dock at the river and he pulls in and parks.

"Mr. Shannon?"

"Yes."

"Good evening, I am Isaac and we have everything taken care of for you. Right this way."

"Thank you Isaac."

I get out the car, trying to figure out what he has cooked up.

"Stop trying to figure it out Camille and just follow Isaac."

"I don't know Isaac."

"But you know me."

"And?"

"Girl, stop playing. I should have blindfolded you."

"Wow! This is beautiful," I say, stepping onto one of the largest boats I've ever seen. It was decked out on the inside. I mean absolutely amazing. "It smells great in here."

"That would be thanks to our chef for tonight."

"Good evening Judge Cam."

"Todd? Chloe, Ray, Shelby, Brian, Kerri, Mike, Paul and Anthony! Oh my God! How?"

"Your husband with Anthony and Ray's help, pulled all of this together," Shelby says.

"Just a way to congratulate you on becoming Judge Camille Shannon; we are proud of you girl," Ray says, smiling.

"Where is Lyn? Has anyone talked to her?"

"She said she was coming," Paul said.

"Well, I am just glad all of you are here. Thank you. I cannot be who I am without the support system I have in all of you. Each of you love me, flaws and all, and I cannot thank you enough for that. I don't know what lies ahead of this new journey, but I need each of you on the ride. I love you guys."

"We love you too. Let's eat!"

\*\*\*

After spending a few hours with the gang, we finally make it home. We check in on

183

the kids, who were asleep and for once in a long time, I truly enjoyed hanging with my husband.

Finally making it to our bedroom, I pull him into a hug.

"Thank you for an amazing night."

"You deserved it."

"But after everything we've been dealing with and going through, you didn't have to do it."

"After everything we've been dealing with and been through, I had to do it."

I lean in to kiss him. I let my tongue connect with his, because I need to feel him. I grab the back of his head and I tongue this man as if it's the last kiss I'll ever give him. I need to feel him in my soul. I've missed him. He removes my jacket and let it fall to the floor. He unzips my skirt and I let it slide to the floor. I step back from him, he unbuttons my shirt and it falls to the floor. I turn around, he unfastens my bra and it falls to the floor. He pushes my thongs down and they fall to the floor at my ankles. I still have on my stilettos. He likes me to keep them on.

"Damn, I love your body," he says, as he runs his hand from my chest down to my belly button.

He takes my hand and leads me over to the chaise in our room. He sits down and tells me to stand in front of him. He puts one of my legs up and places my hands on his shoulders. He slowly blows on my clit, before taking her into his mouth.

"Oooh," I moan.

He licks, slowly. He's taking his time as if they are just meeting for the first time. I try moving my hips, gyrating to let him know I need him to speed up, but he grabs my waist to make me stop. He's in control. I like this. He licks some more, using all of his tongue. I bend over a little, because this shit is feeling too good. He enters a finger into me, his middle finger and he is rubbing it back and forth, slowly.

"Oh!"

I am extremely wet; it's running down my leg. I want to put my hand down there and help him pick up the pace, but he won't let me. He's enjoying this. I am too.

"I'm cumming," I moan to him as he inserts another finger into me, sucking harder on my clit.

He moves back to undress, which is the only thing he does quickly. He turns around on the chaise and I mount him, taking all of him into me. I put my legs on both sides of the chaise, both feet on the floor, which allows me to ride him. I grab the back of the chaise and give him all of me. I squeeze my muscles to make sure he feels my pleasure the way I feel him.

"I'm cumming," I say again, picking up my pace, bouncing my ass up and down on him as the orgasm runs through me.

He grabs my waist and flips me back on the chaise, so that he is now on top, with my legs over my head. His paces picks up.

"Right there, harder, yes!" I say, before squirting all over hm.

His pace picks up again, before he releases himself into me. "Damn girl," he says, kissing me. "It's been a long time since I've seen you squirt. That shit is sexy as hell.

"It's been a long time since you have taken the time to take me there," I say, rubbing his back. "Thank you for everything tonight. I really enjoyed it and you."

"You are welcome. I love you, Cam."

"I love you too. Now, move so I can take a shower."

"Let's take one together. Maybe I can see this squirt thing again."

"Oh Lord." I laugh as he pulls me up.

I get up in the middle of the night for a glass of water and I check my phone. There are ten missed calls from Jyema and over twenty text messages. Shit, we were supposed to meet. I start going through some of the text messages and they had me shaking my head. Really?

"Hey. Call me."

"Where are you?"

"Why aren't you answering me?"

"So, you just blow me off?"

"The least you could have done was called. I understand things happen, but you could have called."

"You know what, fuck you! Don't call me again!"

"Damn." I say, before texting her back.

"I apologize for not calling or texting you. Everything happened so fast that I didn't get a chance to. It was not my intention to blow you off. Again, I apologize. I do think it's time we stop seeing each other."

"That's fine. Congratulations by the way."

"Thanks."

# Chapter 37

*2 weeks later – Swearing-In*

The day of the swearing-in was finally here and I am nervous and excited. It is being held at the Shelby County Criminal Justice Complex's auditorium, followed by a reception in Division VII courtroom. My parents, my Aunt Sara and surprisingly, my cousin Reese and her husband Noah, all came up from Miami to be here. All of my girls and their families were here and even Lyn. Mr. Thompson and his wife, Judge Alton, and a few of my co-workers. More people than I can name. What the hell. No, that can't be who I think it is.

Never mind that Cam, shake it off.

Standing here with Thomas and our children, I repeat the oath that will forever change my life...

"I, Camille Holden Shannon, do solemnly swear that I will support the Constitution of the United States of America and the Constitution of the State of Tennessee; that I will administer justice without respect of persons, and that I will faithfully and impartially discharge all the duties incumbent upon me as Judge of the Circuit Court, Seventh Judicial District of

Tennessee, to the best of my skill and ability, so help me God."

I finish the swearing-in process and we move to the reception. I am making my way through the well-wishers, trying to get to Thomas but before I do, I see that he is dragging Chelle's ass out of there. The nerve of that wench.

I look around to see where my parents and kids are when I come eye to eye with my mom, who lets me know she has this covered, so I breathe a sigh of relief.

"I can't seem to get a moment alone with you."

"I know. How are you Charles? Damn, you smell good," I whisper into his ear as I give him a hug of thanks.

"And you are looking good enough to eat. I cannot wait to get you across your new desk," he whispers in my ear.

"What are you two whispering about?" Mr. Thompson asks.

"Just congratulating her."

"You two are coming to the party tonight, right? My mom would be offended if you didn't."

"Of course. You know I owe your mom a dance."

"You owe my wife what?" My dad asks, coming up behind him.

"You heard me, you old fool."

They both break out into a laugh.

"Thompson, thank you for taking care of my baby girl up here in Memphis."

"It has been my pleasure Holden."

"Don't you two start," I say, when I notice Thomas coming back in. "Will you gentlemen excuse me?"

"Babe, what was Chelle doing here?"

"I don't know. She claim there is something you need to know but I told her now was not the place."

"Tell me? About what?"

"I don't know. She was talking crazy about a slide show and some pictures. She wasn't making sense. I told her to go home and we would talk to her after the party."

"Thanks. The last thing I need is her putting on a show here."

"Are you ready to get out of here?"

"Yes, please."

We make it back to my parents and finally find my Aunt Sara, who was laughing in the face of another judge.

I clear my throat to get her attention. "Hmm, excuse me ma'am, but are you ready to go?"

"Girl, can't you see me talking to this fine gentleman?"

"Auntie, this is Judge Christiansen from Division Eight, next door. Why don't you invite him to the party tonight, that way you can save him a dance. I'll be waiting for you by the door."

Now, do you see where I get it from?

# Chapter 38

"You ready for the party?" Thomas asks, walking into the room.

"As ever as I could be. I just can't believe I am now an official judge," I tell him, standing up from my vanity.

"Wow."

"What?"

"You look amazing."

Sam did an amazing job with the dress she sent me. It arrived a few days ago and I hadn't even bothered to try it on, because I knew Sam; she knew my body well. The dress is a black and silver long sheath evening gown that is contoured to my body just right. It's off the shoulder and the back swings low enough to show skin, but still maintain a level of class. I paired it with these black and silver Giuseppe Zanotti Stilettos that fit it perfectly. Yeah, I know. I don't normally spend that much on a pair of shoes, but when I saw these, I had to have them.

"I guess you like the dress."

"Yes. Is it one of Lyn's?"

"No. It's actually one from my friend named Sam from Miami."

"Sam?" He asks, looking confused.

"Yes. She sent it to me; it came the other day. Is everybody ready and is the car here?"

"Oh okay," he replies, when he realizes Sam is a she and not he. "No, it should be here in ten minutes."

"Okay. I am on my way down."

***

We make it to the Hilton where the party is being held. My mom was in charge of course, so she was off handling last minute things in the ballroom. My family was at the bar and the girls hadn't arrived yet. We get there a little earlier, because Thomas and I decide to stay overnight, so we go to check in first. Thomas made sure all our bags and everything were already put away, but we still had time to wait. My mom had an entire program prepared, and I couldn't step one foot in where the party was being held. She had a private area set up for me, so Thomas and I were back there sitting and drinking wine.

"Dang, I left my earrings."

"Where are they, I'll get them." Thomas says, getting up.

"They are in the bag that is inside of my cosmetic bag, inside of—you know what, never mind. I need to freshen up my makeup anyway. I'll be right back. Give me the room key."

"Okay, but don't be long. You know how your mom is. We are set to go into the party in thirty minutes."

"I know."

"Babe, thirty minutes."

"I'll be back in ten, promise."

I make it into the room and it is dark. Dang, why didn't Thomas leave any lights on? As soon as I reach for the light switch, someone starts clapping. "Well bravo, Judge Camille Shannon."

"Who's there?" I ask, because I don't recognize her voice right off.

"They say you can't turn a hoe into a housewife, but I guess you can turn a hoe into a judge, huh?"

"Who are you?" I ask again, this time getting angry.

"Even after everything I did to sabotage you, them motherfuckers still gave you the job and you accepted!"

"I guess you didn't do enough. Look, you may have time to stay here all night, but I have a party to. So, either show yourself, say what you have to say or get the fuck out my room."

"Who said anything about you getting back to the party?"

I start laughing.

"Something funny?" she asks.

"Yes, your sad ass. You've gone through a whole lot to screw me over, and for what? What have I done to you? Did I fuck your husband better than you could, or did I suck your girlfriend's clit so good that she was calling my name at home? And now you've set out on a mission to destroy Camille Shannon. How's that working for you?"

"Fuck you!" she screams.

"Have I or is that what you want?" I say, moving close to her.

"Stop!"

"Or what? Isn't this what you want?" I ask, moving closer to her and rubbing myself. "Wasn't all of this about you getting to me? Here I am, boo."

"Now you want me?" she asked, softening.

I stop. "What do you mean now?"

"Do you want me now Cam?"

"Obviously I don't, or we wouldn't both be here and you wouldn't be working so hard to ruin my life. So, tell me; what did I do or what didn't I do to deserve all this?"

"You don't know?"

"Girl, I don't have time for your games. Show yourself or let me get what I came to get and you can stay here until I get back."

"Or I can go downstairs and ruin your party and your career."

"Go ahead."

She didn't move. I walk towards the bathroom.

"Where are you going?"

"To get my earrings. You've wasted enough of my time with this foolishness."

I go into the bathroom, get my earrings, and fix my lip-gloss. This damn fool is still sitting or standing in the dark when I come out.

"So, what are you going to do? Are you coming to the party or you staying here?"

"You must think you are invincible!"

"No, but I am tired. I am tired of dealing with a coward who calls from a blocked number, who busts windows out of people's cars, who leaves notes on windows, who sends pictures, and calls news stations. I am tired and I am fed up."

"Then why aren't you tired of playing with people's feelings?"

"Stop getting your fucking feelings involved and they won't get hurt."

"You are one cold bitch."

"No, my name is Cam; take me or leave me," I say, walking towards the door.

"Or what?"

"Or I will blow your brains out," she says, turning on the light to reveal a gun pointed directly at me.

I start laughing.

"Why are you laughing?" she asks.

"Because you are one crazy bitch, but I never expected this from you. You did all this after getting your pussy ate a few times? Damn! I knew I was good, but damn!"

"Fuck you Cam! You think you can make people fall in love with you and then you can just walk all over them! Fuck you!"

"Girl, ain't nobody walked over you. You have a husband. You knew what this was before you opened your legs and invited my head in between them, so go on with all that. You got caught up and you know it."

"Caught up?"

"Yes, you got caught up by Ms. Nice Nasty and you couldn't handle it, so you tried to drag my name and career into it, but it backfired on your raggedy ass and since that didn't work, you're going to kill me now?"

"I might."

"Go ahead, but with your track record, you'll miss." I laugh, knowing damn well I am scared as hell.

"You're so sure, huh?" she says, raising the gun as someone uses a key to open the door.

"Babe, your mom is —, what the hell?" Thomas yells as a gunshot rings out!

Also available

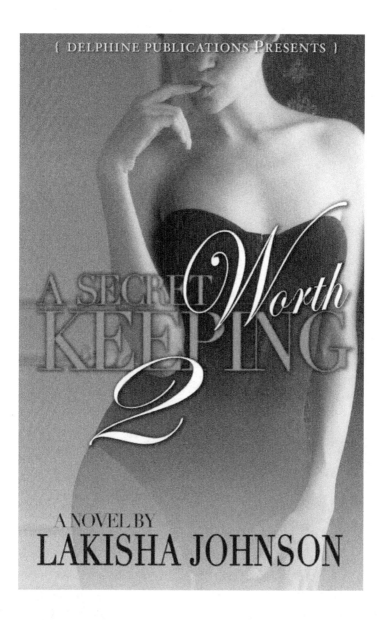

{ DELPHINE PUBLICATIONS PRESENTS }

A SECRET *Worth*
KEEPING
2

A NOVEL BY
LAKISHA JOHNSON

CPSIA information can be obtained at www.ICGtesting.com
Printed in the USA
LVOW04s2135090615

441857LV00013B/147/P